WAHIDA CLARK PRESENTS

W•CLARK
PUBLISHING

DEEPLY ROOTED

A NOVEL BY

ICE MIKE

This is a work of fiction. Names, characters, places, and incidents either are the product of the author's imagination or are used fictitiously, and any resemblance to actual persons, living or dead, business establishments, events, or locales are entirely coincidental.

Wahida Clark Presents Publishing
60 Evergreen Place
Suite 904
East Orange, New Jersey 07018
973-678-9982
www.wclarkpublishing.com

Deeply Rooted by Ice Mike
ISBN 13-digit 978-19366493-7-2
ISBN 10-digit 1936649373

Library of Congress Cataloging-In-Publication Data:
LCCN 2013919947
   1. Crips Bloods 2. Thug Life 3. Thugs 4. Kingpin
   5. Life Sentence Years 6. Robbery 7. Drug dealers
   8. Black Romance Novels

Cover design and layout by Nuance Art, LLC
Book design by Nuance Art, LLC
Proofreader Rosalind Hamilton
Sr. Editor Linda Wilson

Acknowledgements

Before I even dare acknowledge an inkling of my success I first acknowledge You Father God, for it is through Your grace and mercy that I am here today. Thank You for life, thank You for love, thank You for my victories, thank You for my sorrows, thank You for my yesterday's, thank You for my tomorrow's, and thank You for everything else that came along the way, because all that I've ever been through made me who I am today . . .

A special thank you to **Wahida Clark,** for recognizing game and giving me a chance to shine. Words cannot express how truly appreciative I am that you saw through the rough and raw unpolished diamond. Thank you to the entire WCP staff as well, especially you **Sherry, Ne Ne Capri** (priceless advice), and **Hadiyah.** Without ya'll this would still be a dream I'm chasing, not the dream I'm living.

To my mother; I love you more than words can express, its unconditional. To my son **Michael Lamar Davis;** I love you more than I've ever loved me. It is with you in mind that I strive to be a better man every day. Let this be living proof that its never too late to change baby boy, you feel me? I believe in you and know that you will live to do great things, its in our DNA. To my brothers; **Choo Choo** and **Tracy;** I love ya'll, always have and always will! I told you I was gon' blow lil bro!!! To my real potna **Keith Thompson**, my brother from another mother; we've been through a lot of shit together, pains and thangs that the average folk couldn't understand, now its time to Do Tha Damn Thang bruh! To **Dee Dee**; I aint mad atcha, you will always be family to me. To my girl **Co-Co (Faustina Nwozuzu,** my first TRUE friend and a REAL African queen! I love you Black Girl). The Davis Family. The Morris Family. Ebony Darby holla at ya boy.

Thank you to my very first fans, the folks who read my books when they were still in its handwritten form. Ya'll gave me the confidence to go hard with this writing and push my pen without fear of the reaction; **Paul Blue** especially you, Dago love. **Lovely Da' Silverback. Badger. Jiggalow** (keep havin' those billionaire dreams, its in you playa!) To my boy **9-Ball**, keep pokin' holes in that paper with yo' pen because these people need to hear what you have to say. **Jon-Jon. Set-Trip. J.D. Cooper** (yo' pen game is sick bruh!) **B.J** a.ka **ROOTS. Kenny. Technique. C-Bear. Black Tone, C-Mack.** My playa patna from way back in the day **Fela-Tee** (I cant wait for that Diamonds & Thugs to come out; I predict a hood classic! Now grow up so you can blow up! That's real talk bruh bruh . . .) To **Abayomi Brame**, you set a good example bruh and I appreciate the positive advice you provide. To **Margaret White** aka **Ms. Inspiration**, my inspiration. To **Sa'Rese** (Stripping Asjiah I & II), sometimes the truth hurts and your words cut deep, but those wounds healed quick with motivation my medication now look at me!) **To Ms. Shai Sexy,** you know who you are, pick up that pen and quit playin'! It's in you so im a stay on you. I got you if you need me. To young **G'sta**; you got the gift bruh but it aint gon' unwrap itself, you gotta put in the work to make it do what it do. To the chosen few (6-Time Champ!). Amani Ferguson, you know what it is. Holla! **B. Laws. Ms. Dixion. Sherri A.**

If I didn't mention you, or I somehow forgot your name don't blame it on my heart blame it on my brain.

If you were a part of my past and you're not a part of my future then its self-explanatory, you feel me?

To all the folks who ever hated on me; I really aint even mad atcha, I'm just sittin' back LMMFAO atcha! YAH-DA-DA DA-MEAN!!!

To the reader's; if you bought this book then I sincerely thank you from the bottom of my heart. If you become a fan of mines I thank you even more. I invite you all to join me on this journey, enjoy this ride from start to finish, from this first book to my last book. This is just the beginning ya'll, I swear I'ma continue to create hot ass stories and put out bomb ass books for years to come so keep checkin' for ya boy.

Coming Soon: Other books by Ice Mike:

Golden State Heavyweights

Dipped in Chocolate, Vol. 1

Passion Wit' A Pistol

1-4-69 Birth of a Poet

For any comments and/or feed-back holla at ya boy writing me at:

Michael A. Davis

#H-08904

P.O. BOX 2000

Vacaville, Cal. 95696

WAHIDA CLARK PRESENTS

DEEPLY ROOTED

A Novel by

ICE MIKE

PROLOGUE

San Diego, California, 1989

Y ou ma'fuckas need to chill out on all that yip-yappin' and focus on the ma'fuckin' task at hand!" Bojack's booming voice silenced the chitchat. The Russian-made AK-47 he toted emphasized his point. "We shoulda been had all this shit counted up, wrapped, and ready to go by now! As a matter of fact, the next ma'fuckin' one of you I see bumpin' they gums consider ya'self paid because you won't get a ma'fuckin' dime from me!"

For the next two hours, the only sound in the small room was the steady hum of the money machine, constant clicking of calculator keys, and plastic cellophane being wrapped tightly around bundles of money.

"I gotta use the bathroom, Bojack," the slim, baby-faced, young thug said in a tired, almost pleading voice.

"Go 'head, Bad Boy. But first, stand yo' ass up and stretch out. You know the deal. Let me make sho' you ain't clippin' the boss for no cheese, or tryin' no other type of slick shit."

The eighteen year old in charge of wrapping the money in cellophane stood and spread his arms and legs. He had long grown accustomed to the overly cautious Bojack searching him anytime he had to leave his sight in the money house.

Kiko Dunbar had the nigga Bojack spooked to death. Kiko was the biggest dope dealer in San Diego, known for his ruthless and savage way of doing business. Damn near everybody feared Kiko Dunbar. Bad Boy was one of the few who didn't, at least not today.

"Hurry the fuck up, Bad Boy! We just about finished, and Kiko wants this shit loaded up and in traffic before the sun goes down."

"Okay, I'm only gon' be a minute," Bad Boy told Bojack.

Once he shut himself inside the small bathroom, he locked the door and immediately went to work. He stood on the toilet seat and pushed the small window open. Then he reached up and felt around for the line he taped to the wall outside. Bad Boy knew Bojack always searched inside and outside of the house, so yesterday he used clear tape and clear fishing line, and then painted over it to assist in his bold and daring plot. With a kid on the way and another girl possibly pregnant by him, this cheese would set him up and take care of his family in a real way for years to come.

After locating the fishing line, he reached out further and wrapped the line around his four fingers. He pulled hard until finally the 9-millimeter on the opposite end buried just beneath the surface of the soft ground unearthed itself and broke free.

Bang! Bang! Bang! Bang! Bang!

The heavy pounding on the bathroom door spooked the shit out of Bad Boy and almost caused him to drop the fishing line, along with the gun. He held his breath, desperately hoping Bojack wouldn't burst the door open.

"What the fuck is takin' yo' ass so long, nigga?" Bojack demanded. His eyes never strayed from the two girls that he kept in his line of vision at all times.

"Can I wipe my ass, Bojack? I mean, damn, man. It ain't like I'm goin' nowhere." He prayed his response would suffice.

"Hurry the fuck up, fool! They finished with the money. So get yo' ass out here and wrap it up, so we can shake the spot and drop it off!" Bojack knew Bad Boy didn't present any type of threat. He had already thoroughly inspected the entire residence, inside and out for weapons, tape recorders, and any other devices that could get him or his boss sent to the penitentiary or a graveyard forever.

Bad Boy quickly tucked the pistol in his pants and flushed the toilet. He wiped up the bit of dirt that had fallen off the gun and stepped out the bathroom.

He went about wrapping the last stacks of money, and together, he and the two girls who operated the machines packed the dough into some boxes. When they were finished, five boxes containing a total of five million dollars were ready to be loaded into the van parked inside the garage.

Bad Boy hoped like hell that the girls would play their positions as planned. He made eye contact with them both, confident that all was well.

"Ai'ight now, each one of y'all grab a box and follow that nigga Bad Boy to the van," Bojack instructed, using the AK to direct traffic. The two girls did as told, and as planned, the younger of the two dropped the box she was holding.

"Dang Bojack, I can't carry that heavy ass box by myself all the way over there," she cried as she struggled with the box.

"If you don't knock it the fuck off and pick up that fuckin' box, then you damn sho' ain't finna pick up no paycheck!" Bojack barked.

"It's too heavy!" She maintained her position, hands on hips, lips pouting, while her neck rotated in a slow circle.

Bojack turned to confront the uncooperative girl. That's when he slipped and gave Bad Boy the opening he had been waiting for.

Pop! Pop! Pop!

The 9-millimeter sounded off like three loud firecrackers echoing loudly in the close confines. Each bullet hit its target and peppered Bojack's chest.

The 6-feet 4-inches tall Hulk staggered back from the impact of the gunfire, his face a mask of shocked disbelief. Involuntarily, he squeezed the AK's trigger.

Yopp! Yopp! Yopp! Yopp! Yopp!

The explosive burst of spray hit the two girls in the chest and face, laying them down instantly.

Bad Boy ducked out of the way, trying to avoid the unexpected erratic outburst from the assault rifle.

"You lil bitch ass nigga!" Bojack hollered as he began to recover from the initial shock of getting busted on. The bulletproof vest absorbed all three shots from the 9-millimeter. The thumping hot pain against his chest was nothing in comparison to the heated anger he felt. *The nerve of this young nigga trying to make a power move on me!* He swung the AK-47 toward the bold, baby-faced thug.

I C E M I K E

Pop!

But it was too late.

Bad Boy stood stone-faced, arm out-stretched with the pistol aimed at Bojack. A wisp of gray smoke curled up and twisted into a vanishing column at the end of the barrel.

A single bullet hit Bojack in the left eye and splattered his blood and the back of his head against the wall behind him. He fell backward with his finger on the trigger. The AK-47 sounded off and sent finger-thick bullets into the ceiling.

Yopp! Yopp! Yopp! Yopp! Yopp!

Bad Boy casually stepped over Bojack's now frozen frame and tiptoed around the two girls twisted up bodies. He shook his head sadly and felt a twinge of pain for his young cohorts. *Sorry it went down like that, y'all,* he thought before he bent down and picked up the first box of money. *But on the real, though, that's two less people I gotta split this money with.* Quickly, he carried each of the five boxes to the Nissan Maxima that sat parked at the curb in front of the stash house.

An hour later, he was in his mother's backyard under the cover of darkness with a shovel in his hands. It was an all-night affair, but when it was all said and done, Bad Boy had managed to bury the entire five million dollars under the lemon tree next to the fence.

* * * * *

If you want something done right you gotta do the damn thang yourself! Kiko Dunbar thought angrily. He leaned forward over the steering wheel, peering hard into the gloomy gray morning in search of the four-digit address on the small slip of paper in his hand. *That lil bitch ass nigga*

DEEPLY ROOTED

Bad Boy is a dead man when I catch up to him. Think he gon' take money from Kiko Dunbar and get away with it. Nigga got me fucked up! His foot tapped lightly on the gas as the big body Blazer crept slowly down the block.

Halfway down the street, Kiko smiled for the first time since discovering his money house had been hit for five million dollars. "I see yo' bitch ass," he whispered when he spotted Bad Boy walking hurriedly toward the black Nissan Maxima. Kiko slowed to a stop about thirty yards away and let the Nissan jump into traffic, and then push down the street. After a couple of right turns, he reached for the sawed-off twelve-gauge pump and set the heavy murder weapon in his lap.

* * * * *

Bad Boy saw the Blazer out the corner of his eye when he stuck the key into the ignition. *That gotta be Kiko's people!* The thought raced through his amped up, paranoid mind. He twisted the key and desperately tried to put as much distance between himself and his mother's house, as well as the freshly buried five million under the lemon tree.

A couple of blocks later, as he sat idling at a stop sign, Bad Boy's eyes bugged wide, and his heart rate accelerated. The Blazer suddenly came barreling down on the Maxima. He threw the Nissan in reverse and smashed on the gas. When the two vehicles collided, it sounded like a small explosion on the quiet street.

The counter-move caught the kingpin by surprise. His gun fell to the floor near his feet. When he came back up with the sawed-off shotty, his eyes were as big as golf balls.

7

Bad Boy walked toward him with a mean-mug and a 9-millimeter in his outstretched hand.

The lil nigga got the drop on me, Kiko admitted the obvious. His ugly reality played out in slow motion right before his terrified eyes.

Pop! Pop! Pop! Pop! Pop! Pop! Pop!

Bad Boy emptied the clip on the kingpin. Seconds later, when cop cars came screeching around the corner, Bad Boy knew his capture was inevitable. He resigned himself to the possibility that he may never get an opportunity to spend a dollar of the hard-earned stolen cash.

Instead, twenty-three years later, another generation of thugs would be left to reap the rewards of his gangsta.

DEEPLY ROOTED

CHAPTER ONE
Five Million Dollar Mystery

Wicked

Present day . . . February 2012

Wicked's cold, black eyes traced along one of the many crooked lines that ran like a panicked maze across the ceiling's expanse. He lay sprawled out on his back across the king-sized bed and stared up at the cracked white ceiling. The early morning sun beamed brightly through the bedroom curtains, invading the otherwise darkened cavern that was the thug's lair. Unsettled dust particles danced energetically in the beams of light provided by the sun's incessant shine.

Blinking his eyes several times, Wicked took a deep breath and reached down to caress his morning fresh erection. He slowly exhaled and closed his eyes again, trying his damnedest to recapture the freaky dream that had him on brick first thing in the morning. Unable to do so, he opened his eyes and stretched his muscular built, heavily tattooed frame to its limits with a deep yawn. His elbow rubbed up against the softness that occupied the space next to him, which caused him to look to his left.

Immediately, thoughts of last night's raunchy sex session with the beautiful, voluptuous hood rat flooded his mind. A smile slowly formed on his handsome, chocolate brown face. He palmed his erection again. "I guess it wasn't a dream after all," he muttered before he snatched the sheet back and tossed it toward the foot of the bed.

"Huh? Whatchu' say, boo?" the soft voice next to him sleepily asked. Her green-eyes remained shut as she tried to snuggle up close to him in search of warmth. Her firm, jiggly tits against his torso did it. He rose up and mounted her from the rear as she now lay face down. Her round ass poked out like a small beach ball. Slowly, he slid his long, thick, love muscle deep into her warm, wet slit and took pleasure at the soft moans that repeatedly escaped her full lips. He slow stroked the pussy with deep methodical motions that touched every one of her walls.

"Ooh shit! That feels sooo damn good," she cried out into the plush mattress beneath her. He had only been out of prison two weeks now, and his pipe was still as hard as the penitentiary steel that had confined him for the past four years.

He continued to stab her wet softness with long, slow measured strokes that never seemed to pause or stop, until eventually, it became too much for the high-yellow beauty to resist. She pushed back at him, trying to meet his pleasure pounding in the middle. This only made Wicked bang up in it harder, faster, and deeper. It wasn't long before her meaty ass cheeks were slapping loudly against his pelvic area. A squishing noise followed each violent thrust of his hips; the clapping sound was straight up sex music.

After twenty minutes of unbridled, thuggish thumping inside her silken softness, Wicked buried his donkey meat as deep as it would go and released a couple of thick spurts of hot nut into the recesses of her sugary walls. Beneath him, her entire body shook hard from her own orgasm. Only then did he extract his swollen member. Wicked rolled onto his back and reached for the kush-filled blunt that sat in the ashtray.

"Suck on me, Jracia, while I blaze this bomb ass bush, ai'ight?"

"Fo' sho'," was all the sex kitten said as she positioned herself between his hairy, muscular thighs and went to work. She devoured his dick and deep-throated his length with skill until he finally erupted a second time in the back of her mouth.

When she came up off his now softening swipe, he passed her what remained of the blunt.

"I'm finna jump in the shower before I bounce up outta here and go handle some bizness, baby. Hook me up a lil somethin' to grub on before I cut out," he told her as he stepped toward the bathroom.

"Sausage, hash browns, and eggs?" Jracia asked with her eyes closed. She squeezed her thighs together with a smile plastered all over her face.

"Yeah, that's cool," he hollered back seconds later over the noise of the cascading shower spray. Wicked stepped under the hot, jetting water, letting it wash over his sex soaked skin. He closed his eyes, bowed his head, and allowed himself to become lost in his thoughts. His mind flashed back to a conversation he had with his prison cellmate, an older thug who had caught an "L" for killing a man long before he had ever been born.

"Young Wicked, you wouldn't believe it if I told you that you was talkin' to a multi-millionaire ma'fucka, would you?" The forty-one-year-old OG coughed into his hand. "If you just looked around this cell and took inventory of what lil property I have, you would think that you was livin'

wit' a old broke, sick dude that won't stop with the coughin', huh?" he said with a wave of his hand. Another fit of coughing violently wracked his body.

"Damn, Ol' School. Is you okay?" Wicked asked his older cellie, concerned because the brotha he shared a cell with for two years now was getting sicker by the day. "Why don't you go see a doctor or somethin', bro? For real, Ol' School. You really starting to sound bad."

"I done told you before, Young Wicked. I ain't fuckin' wit' them white folks no mo'. Shit, as far as I'm concerned, it was them dirty ma'fuckas who got me sick like this in the first place." Another bout of coughing rattled the older thug's now fragile frame.

"Them white folks ain't give you cancer, Ol' School. You don't catch that. You just get it."

"Nigga, I know that!" the older thug roared angrily. Another bout of coughing bent him in half with chest pain. "I never said they gave it to me. I said it was them white folks who got me sick like this!"

"How you figure that, Ol' School?" Wicked wasn't tripping on his cellie getting loud and agitated with him. He knew it was simply his anger at his circumstances that made him hot like that. Ol' School was about the same age he guessed his pops would be. In reality, that wasn't old at all, but the cancer that had slowly ravaged his body had him looking twice the age of a forty-one year old. He was definitely on his last leg.

"Because them fake, wack ass doctors misdiagnosed my illness, Young Wicked. They shoulda detected this cancer when it first surfaced. When it coulda been treated and eradicated from my body. But instead of diagnosing me with *cancer like they was supposed to do, they dropped the ball and said it wasn't shit but a bad cold. Then they said it was walkin' pneumonia, man. Them punk ma'fuckas practically killed me!" The older thug breathed in and out heavily as anger consumed him. He wheezed loudly before coughing again. The blood on his handkerchief wasn't new to him. He knew he didn't have much longer. That's why the secret that had lain buried in the deepest recesses of his mind was fighting to come out, like a death bed confession of sorts. "You never did answer my question, Young Wicked," he said after the coughing subsided and he regained his composure.*

"What question is that, Ol' School?" Wicked referred to the older thug by the nickname he had grown used to calling him.

"I said you wouldn't believe it if I told you that you was sittin' here talkin' to a multi-millionaire, would you?"

Wicked looked at him like he was stupid and smiled. "Hell naw! Why the fuck would I believe some shit like that? I mean, you hardly ever get a package or go to the commissary since I been here, bruh. And you ain't got no millions hidden up in your property, unless I'm missing something. So naw, I wouldn't believe you if you told me you was a multi-millionaire!"

Wicked wasn't one to bite his tongue, so it was nothing for him to tell the truth about whatever, despite his cellmate's condition.

"Well, you need to take a good long look at me, Young Wicked, because as sure as our black asses is locked up in this maximum security prison, I am a millionaire. Five times over!" The older thug seemed to get lost in his thoughts, dreaming with his eyes wide open.

DEEPLY ROOTED

Having nothing better to do, Wicked decided to entertain his cellie. "If you're a millionaire, Ol' School, then where is all your money? Where is all this loot you keep speakin' on?"

The question shook the older thug out of the twenty-three year long recurring reverie, and he snapped to the here and now. He let his piercing brown eyes bore into his young cellmate's cold, black eyes before speaking. "Under the lemon tree, Young Wicked. The money is all up under the lemon tree." No sooner were the words out of his mouth did the older thug erupt into a loud horror show type laughter.

Wicked thought there was something eerily chilling about his laugh. He held the stare with his cellie for as long as he could, only breaking it after the older thug started coughing again.

"Is that right, Ol' School? For real?" Wicked asked as he rose up from the stool he had been sitting on. He jumped up onto his top bunk with the weirdest feeling eating at him. The feeling of, What if the dying thug wasn't lying after all? It was rumored that he caught his life sentence for murdering a kingpin named Kiko Dunbar, after robbing him for a grip of money. The rumors never made mention of the amount of money he had jacked Kiko Dunbar for. Maybe nobody knew the actual amount. Maybe the actual amount was five million dollars just like Ol' School had said. Those were his words: "I am a millionaire. Five times over!"

That was the last time he had ever spoken to his cellie. The next morning during chow call, Ol' School fell out on the yard and was taken to the prison hospital. From what Wicked was able to gather before he paroled, Ol' School or Bad Boy, which was his real nickname, received one final visit from his mother before his ticker stopped and he flat lined. He had fought the deadly cancer like a true soldier to the end. Never once did he take any pain medication to ease his suffering. Bad Boy died a slow, painful death, and Wicked was right there to witness it all up until the end.

With two weeks to the house, Bad Boy's death made Wicked appreciate his life that much more. He soaped up and rinsed off before finally stepping out of the shower, dripping wet and naked. He dried off and threw on a pair of baggy Red Monkey jeans with a form-fitting wife beater, followed by a crisp white tee. He stepped into a fresh pair of white-on-white Air Force One's and went to see about breakfast. The smell coming from the kitchen was teasing the hell out of his appetite. Jracia could cook her fine, thick ass off.

Wicked shook off the chills that ran throughout his body when he thought of the possibility of five million dollars actually being buried up under a lemon tree somewhere in Southeast San Diego, a mystery he was dead set on solving.

DEEPLY ROOTED

CHAPTER TWO
Point of No Return

Wahdatah

W
e were at the point of no return. The minute I pulled my thumper out, all hell was gone break loose. Wasn't no turning back. I was committed to carrying out this gangsta shit. It was do or die in my eyes. Get paid or get popped trying. I ain't gone lie, I was nervous as fuck! My legs shook like a minibike, and my heart pounded harder than a Dr. Dre beat. My palms were sweating so much I had to keep wiping them down on my three-piece.

I looked around the joint and made sure everything was good. Moolah was in position, playing his role to perfection. Thun-Thun was on the opposite side of the room doing the same. They were both waiting on me. The moment of truth was upon us.

Ai'ight, here it go. It's now or never!

I reached up under the chocolate brown, silk, pinstripe Sean John suit jacket and pulled out the heavy chrome hand canon. Out of my peripheral, I peeped my nigga Moolah come up with the pistol grip pump. I didn't even have to look over to see if Thun-Thun had his twin Glocks up and aimed. He was gung-ho with his pistol play.

My voice was clear and commanding. The sight of the .45 Desert Eagle told everybody in this jewelry store that this wasn't no bullshit.

"Listen the fuck up, or get laid the fuck down! If you sound the alarm and the police show up, er'body in this bitch die! This is a ma'fuckin' robbery, people. So get flat on your face right where the fuck you at, or I'ma start puttin' holes in you. Get the fuck down, ma'fuckas! Now!" I yelled over the chaos that ensued when them white folks saw this big ass pistol waving around and realized their beautiful day had just become ugly. I mobbed toward the glass counter top, and in one smooth, fluid motion I was on the other side of it. The two bitches regulating the cash register and working the counter were stretched out on the floor crying a river and shivering like they were lying on a slab of ice.

"Stand the fuck up, 'ho!" I ordered the brunette chick. The tip of my pistol touched her temple. Her make-up was fucking her face up now, and I swear the bitch was shaking so hard it looked like she was pop locking. "Open er' one of these ma'fuckin' windows, and don't do no dumb shit, or I'ma splash yo' shit all over this glass, ya feel me?" My question was a statement.

The brunette chick was so shook up she couldn't even speak, but nodded emphatically.

The homie Moolah walked over to us and laid down the briefcase that had concealed his gun. The pistol grip pump looked hella goonish in his hand. He swung that ma'fucka around and started issuing out instructions to the other customers in the joint. Two couples lay side by side, and two chicks had their noses pressed hard to the floor.

ICE MIKE

One by one, he accosted them with the shotty pointed in their direction. He emptied pockets, purses, and relieved them of cell phones and car keys, or anything else that could assist in them following us, or getting us cracked by the po-po.

Thun-Thun was near the door patrolling the entrance in case somebody stepped their unlucky ass into the jewelry store. He also had the best view of the entire floor. So if a ma'fucka wanted to be on some hero shit, then he could clack they ass out.

It took a few minutes, but eventually the briefcase was full of bling. That real shit! Every type of ring, watch, bracelet, or chain you could think of. The metallic briefcase weighed hella heavy in my hands. But this ain't what we came for.

"Get yo' ass up!" I told the other broad. I marched both of them bitches to the back. The fear in their eyes oddly gave me more confidence with every step I took. I was sure we could get away with this caper without killing anybody.

"I want the diamond stash!" I snatched the brunette girl's co-worker by her blonde locks and stuck the pistol in her ear. "Don't play no games, bitch. Gimme the ma'fuckin' diamonds, or I'ma murder this 'ho! I swear I'ma splash her noodles all over your punk ass if I don't see the diamonds in front of me in five seconds!"

"Five-four-three-two . . ." I began my countdown.

"Okay, okay, okay, stop!" the brunette bitch cried. A velvet sack of diamonds of all sizes was in my hands before I finished my countdown.

But I still wasn't satisfied.

DEEPLY ROOTED

"I want the rest of the stash too! What? You ain't think I know about that wall safe!" I flung the blonde across the room, and she bounced off the wall before she crumbled to the floor. With lightning quick speed, I wrapped the brunette's long hair around my fist and moved closer till my lips touched her earlobe. "Give me the rest of the diamonds in that wall or die!" I whispered hotly against her ear and stuffed the chrome between her lips.

She mumbled some incoherent shit on the tip of my gun.

In less than a minute, I had the mother lode in my hand. I pulled out two pair of plastic zip ties and cuffed them 'hos to the tower cabinet on the wall by the window.

"Let's bounce!" I told Moolah and Thun-Thun as I hopped back over the counter. I had a briefcase full of jewelry and a shit load of diamonds in my possession. The mission was a success thus far. Now came the hard part—the getaway.

"What the fuck is you lookin' at, punk?" My boy Thun-Thun was on one. He was hella trigger happy, and I could tell he was turnt the fuck up right now. He walked over to one of the dudes lying stretched out on the ground and stepped on his jaw. "Fuck you keep peekin' over here at me for? You tryin' to memorize my face or somethin'? Huh!" he asked and booted him in the temple.

Dude couldn't even answer the questions. It was lights out after that boot to the brain. The others on the floor gasped and cried out after he bapped dude with his Timbos.

"Chill on that extra shit, bro. We tryin' to get up outta here without killin' anybody. Besides, we got er'thang we came for, so let's be out this bitch after we zip these ma'fuckas up."

ICE MIKE

Ten minutes later, everybody was zip tied to something, and we were on our way out the door. I flipped the CLOSED sign on the door on my way out.

With the briefcase in one hand swinging nonchalantly at my leg, and the chrome .45 now in my waistband, I looked every bit the part of a businessman closing up his establishment for the day.

Moolah and Thun-Thun were already at the getaway car when I turned the corner. It was how we had planned it in the event the cops were alerted. They would take off and be the diversion, allowing me to escape with the jewels. The keys were in the visor. The jewels would help retain a good lawyer if they got caught up. Besides, I was the one who had the connect, a Sicilian named Joey Cheese who had mob connections. I was sure of it. The sweat-suit wearing, gold-chain sporting ma'fucka looked like one of them old school mafia cats in *Goodfellas*.

I didn't feel right when I approached the car. Something deep inside my gut was twisting up and telling me that shit wasn't right. I didn't know what it was. I just knew my instincts were telling me that this shit had gone entirely too smooth for my liking.

"Somethin' ain't sittin' right with me, y'all. C'mon, let's go to plan B," I said quietly after I reached the driver's side door. I casually surveyed the scene, but I didn't see anything out of the ordinary.

"Man, get yo' nervous ass in the car and let's get the fuck up outta here, bruh. You trippin' for real, Wahdatah," Moolah joked, slamming the passenger side door.

"I know, man. Let's bounce and get the fuck on before the law really do show up," Thun-Thun said from the backseat.

"Naw, I'm tellin' y'all. Somethin' ain't feelin' right!" I said with renewed energy. Butterflies in my stomach were going crazy. My instincts were on high alert. The butterflies felt more like humming birds now. Before another word could be spoken, shit got ugly.

A bullet shattered the windshield in front of me, hitting the homie Moolah in the eye.

"Oh fuck!" I hollered and ducked inside the car, then twisted the ignition. I mashed on the gas after I yanked on the gear.

"What the fuck was that?" Thun-Thun held both Glocks up with his head near his knees. "Where the fuck did that shit come from, Wahdatah?" He was shook the fuck up in a real way.

I rammed a Benz in front of me, and then pulled on the steering wheel until the getaway car was on top of a curb plowing over some bushes and shrubbery. Another gunshot rang out and exploded against the car's body, and then another.

Boom! Ping . . . Boom! Ping . . .

I hit six or seven more cars before punching it out of the parking lot and turning onto the main street.

"I think we got away! I think we got away!" Thun-Thun sat straight up and looked at Moolah's head. The look on his face showed uncut fear. It didn't matter how hard he tried to keep his gangsta together, this unexpected turn of events had a nigga shook and adrenaline flowing! I swerved to avoid hitting the slow ass car in front of me.

"I told you, nigga! I told you, nigga! I was feelin' bad vibes back there!" I screamed. I can't lie though, I was hella shook the fuck up too.

Then I heard that boom again.

Boom! Thwack! Umph!

Thun-Thun's forehead smacked the headrest hard. I heard him gurgle and choke, and then give a wet cough. His body fell to the side, and he lay dead on the backseat.

I snuck a peek in the rear and that thunderous boom sounded off again.

Boom! Smack!

The rearview mirror shattered to pieces after a bullet smashed into it. Just before the mirror disintegrated, I caught a glimpse of a ma'fucka in a uniform half squatting in the middle of the street taking aim at the getaway car. I had to get off that street!

I banked a hard right at the next side street and gunned the Camaro as fast as I could. Half the windows were shot out. Two dead bodies were in the car with me, and I could hear them sirens wailing off in the distance. They were growing louder and louder. I drove like a mad man for a few minutes. *I gotta get rid of this car!*

Damn man, it wasn't supposed to go down like this! My heart raced and sweat poured down my face like a runaway slave. I forced myself to look to my right, and I almost lost control of the Camaro. My nigga Moolah's eye socket was a hole, and the back of his head was wide the fuck open!

What the fuck kinda gun was that fool shootin'!

My heart stopped beating for a second when I heard that ghetto bird. *Oh fuck! My ass is out if that helicopter get a bead on my whereabouts.*

I slowed the whip down and came to a stop under a carport in the alley. After I popped the briefcase and put the pistol grip pump and two Glocks inside, I snatched out a rag from the trunk and wiped down the steering wheel, and everything else I touched. Then I pulled off the fake beard and tore the mustache off my face. I looked around for a place to hide that shit and ended up burying it under a small mound of dirt. Finally, I wiped my hands off and pulled out my phone.

"It's all bad, Drape! Shit went all bad!" I yelled into the cell.

"What the fuck happened, man!" My right hand man Drape yelled back. I could hear the panic in his voice, and for some odd reason that seemed to calm me down.

"It got ugly, Drape. I don't know how, but somebody peeped us after we broke out. We was outta there! Moolah and Thun-Thun are dead, bro!"

"What!" His reply was high pitched.

"Yup, they both took shots to the head, and they in the car. They done," I told him.

"That's not good, homie. That's not good at all. What about you? Is you good, Wah?" Drape asked me.

"I'm straight, bruh. I got the diamonds, and I'm still alive. And as long as I got these thumpers, nigga, I'ma free man wit' a fightin' chance."

He paused for a minute before he responded. "Where you at, bro? Want me to scoop you up?"

"I'm over here in East Dago. Somewhere on 36th off of El Cajon, I think." I could've sworn that was the last street I turned down before I ducked into the alley. I couldn't be sure. Them gunshots distracted my focus.

"I'm sendin' the home girl Silky over there," he said before I stopped him.

"Naw, naw, don't trip. I see a cab right over here. I'ma hop in that ma'fucka and head yo' way. I should be over there in a half hour or so." I was already headed toward the taxicab.

"Ai'ight then, bro. Be careful, my nig."

"All the time," I responded and walked briskly toward the yellow cab.

A flash of red caught the corner of my eyes, and I instinctively reached for my chrome. My hand eased up on the grip of the .45 when the sexiest woman I'd ever seen came rushing to the cab. Then my mind clicked: *Oh shit! I need to be in that taxi!*

DEEPLY ROOTED

CHAPTER THREE
A Whole 'Nother Level

Wahdatah

U m, excuse me, but I called for this cab, sir," the tall chick in the red dress said hotly, attitude oozing from her aura. But then her angry eyes softened as she took in my appearance. I was used to having that effect on a woman, so I turned up the charm.

"Hey, hey, no need for violence, ma." I threw my hands up in mock surrender and hit her with a Colgate smile, displaying both dimples. "I wasn't tryin' to jack you for your ride, lady." My eyes devoured her curvaceous frame before I came back to rest on her mesmerizing hazel eyes. "I was simply hoping that a brotha could appeal to your softer side, and possibly catch a ride with you." I licked my lips like LL Cool J, and made the dimples deeper with a wider smile. After a quick glimpse into the sky, I saw the helicopter in the distance; it was the size of a fly. I forced myself to relax a little; it was obvious the cops were looking in the wrong area at that moment. I had a little time to work on her, but not much. Po-po was comin' and I wasn't trying to be there when they showed up. But at the same time, I knew that if I acted paranoid or spooked in front of her or the cab driver, it could raise suspicions later. I played it cool, like I didn't have a care in the world. I doubt she even noticed.

"I got somewhere I need to be though," she stated. Although her attitude softened a taste, she wasn't budging. Her hand gripped the door handle in a chokehold.

"And I'm good with that, ma. As a matter of fact, how about we go wherever it is you are going, and I pay for the fare?"

"I don't know . . ." She hesitated. But I felt her giving in, so I pushed a bit further, but kept it gangsta.

"Not only will I pay for the fare, beautiful brown-skinned sistah, but I'll also pay for dinner as well, if you'll kindly accept my offer. It would be my pleasure, to say the least." Again, I looked up and searched the skies.

She bit her bottom lip and tried to suppress the smile forcing its way onto her face. Her eyes brightened with added interest; curiosity was killing her cat. Baby girl in the red dress was eating that shit up like a hungry hostage.

I popped my arm out and looked at the Rolex like I was pressed for time. She peeped it on my wrist just as planned. My gift of gab and the Rolex must have been enough. We were in the backseat exchanging information like it was nothing. During the entire drive, we conversed and discovered that we actually had a few things in common. I told her a little about me, and in turn, she told me a bit about herself.

In the course of that thirty minute time frame, I learned amongst other things that the tall, hazel-eyed, brown-skinned honey's name was Tocarra Rhodes-Robinson. She was a twenty-nine-year-old realtor, single, no kids and currently working on her third novel.

Yeah, she wrote urban fiction. No doubt about it, I had a few real life experiences that she could write a book or two about. Shit, I was literally in the middle of one as we spoke.

We had a dinner date set for Friday night. *I'm definitely hittin' that!*

As previously agreed upon, the cabbie dropped her off, and I paid her fare. The look she gave me before she closed the door let me know the pussy was mine for the taking.

The cab ride took longer than expected to get to my boy Drape's crib, but eventually I got there. Drape was on house arrest, and he had to wear one of those ankle bracelets. So it was impossible for him to go on the lick with us. He had to wear that shit for another thirty days until his house arrest was up.

Being on house arrest might have saved his life today, because normally he would roll with us and drive the car. That was his thing; his driving skills were unmatched.

I paid the taxicab driver and stepped out onto the sidewalk that led up to his house. The sun beamed down on my face hella hard. I unbuttoned the suit jacket and put my hand on the .45. Drape stayed in the heart of Lincoln Park, a violent ass neighborhood, and I was toting a grip worth of jewels. *I don't give a fuck. I'ma shoot anything that even look like a threat to me.*

Thoughts of my homies Moolah and Thun-Thun crowded my mind and fucked with my mental. I grew up with them niggas and had mad love for they ass. It pained me to my core to know they would never live to see another day. I blinked back tears as I jogged up the flight of steps that led to Drape's apartment. Before my knuckles hit the wood, the door opened and I stood eyes to eyes with the cleanest looking gangsta I knew.

"What the fuck happened?" were the first words out of his mouth. He poured two drinks and handed me one.

I plopped down and sank into the soft leather couch, and then sipped my drink. The strong dark liquid burned a trail down my throat and relaxed me.

"I don't know what the fuck happened, man! We went up in there just like we planned, no problems or nothin', Drape! We was out that bitch in fifteen minutes! We tied everybody up before we left, and we was in the car about to bounce. My gut was screamin' that somethin' wasn't right, and then boom! A shot blurked the homie Moolah—hit him in the eye and exploded his dome." I paused to sip the glass of Henny, and he broke in with a question.

"Did you see who bapped him?"

"Naw, bruh. It was so sudden nobody saw it comin'. Then, when I got the fuck up outta there, we was doin' about seventy on a straightaway in traffic. And then Thun-Thun got it in the back of the head. I caught a glimpse of the ma'fucka in the rearview before his bitch ass blasted that too. I saw a fool in a uniform. It looked like a police uniform or a security guard." I downed my drink, and he poured me another.

"That's fuckin' crazy, Wah! It wasn't supposed to go down like that." I saw the tears well up in his eyes.

I buried my head in my hands and allowed my emotions to surface. I openly shed tears for Moolah and Thun-Thun, two real gangstas who I had grown up with. Goon niggas. Good dudes. Two of my closest friends.

Drape fired up a blunt. For the next few hours we just smoked, drank, and reminisced about all the memories we shared growing up and grinding it out in these savage Southeast streets.

"It's a damn shame, Drape!"

"What's that?" he asked from behind a cloud of kush smoke.

"This was supposed to be the lick that took us out the hood life and put us in a position to live the good life." I finally gave the briefcase some attention. I popped it open and set it on the table.

Diamonds of every shape, size, and color winked at us and blinged brilliantly in the dimly lit room. Gold and platinum wrapped around er'thang. For a few seconds we just stared in awe at the sight before us.

"Drape, do you know how muthafuckin' rich we about to be!" I said after I finally shook myself from the trance I had been in and dug my hands into the mountain of exquisite richness.

"Wow! This is the most beautiful-est shit I ever seen, blood!" Drape's eyes were stuck on the open briefcase.

"Let's separate this shit and then split it in half, bruh. Right down the ma'fuckin' middle!" I told him. Together, we started putting everything in its rightful pile. Rings, watches, chains, bracelets, and earrings.

After putting all the jewelry in its respective piles and bagging it all up, I cleared the table off and pulled one of the velvet bags out of my pocket.

"What the fuck?" Drape was confused and curious.

I poured the loose diamonds onto the glass tabletop and heard him catch his breath with disbelief as the stones clinked and made beautiful music. Resting there on the glass was a handful of diamonds, ranging in size from a kernel of corn to the size of a marble.

"You know the only thing better than that right there, my nigga?" I looked up and smiled at him. The look on his face was priceless.

"I-I-I don't even know how to respond to that," he stammered, with his eyes still glued to the diamonds.

"Twice as many, my nigga!" I poured the other bag of stones onto the glass tabletop.

After we got over the initial shock of it all, we split the diamonds into groups according to their sizes. It was like bagging up rocks on a whole 'nother level. I needed to holler at Joey Cheese, my contact, so I could turn this shiny shit into paper.

I'd done my share of robberies before, but never anything this major. So I had to approach this shit from a whole 'nother angle. With the homies Moolah and Thun-Thun down for the count, and my road dawg Drape still on house arrest wearing that ankle bracelet, not to mention the heat on a ma'fucka at the time, it was a must that I lay low and chill for a minute.

Drape and I decided to take the bulk of the jewelry and sell it all in one whop at a flat non-negotiable price. There was at least three million dollars worth of bling, including the diamonds, so we were going to shoot for at least one million, take it or leave it. But I couldn't go see Joey Cheese without back up, so until my boy Drape got off house arrest, we decided to just lean back and lay in the cut. When the time was right we'd make our move.

CHAPTER FOUR
If it's Meant to be . . .

Wahdatah

Although I still wasn't sure who was responsible for shooting Thun-Thun and Moolah, I was sure my two homies would never see the light of day again. A week went by before they were finally put in the ground. It was hard seeing them buried like that. I loved my homies like brothers, but I couldn't mourn forever. In this cruel world life goes on. So I figured now would be as good a time as any to go see about the sexy, hazel-eyed honey, Tocarra. Baby had the type of body that I wanted to explore at my leisure. The fact that she was ambitious and driven only added to my attraction. At twenty-nine she seemed to really have her shit together. It was exactly what my wild ass needed to slow me down.

For our first date, I settled on a black Brioni silk suit with a baby blue shirt, powder blue and black striped silk tie, and a pair of platinum cuff links that vibed with the Rolex. A fresh pair of black gators completed my 'fit. Gazing into the full-length mirror, I looked like a million bucks. Felt like a million bucks. Shit, I was worth a million bucks!

You never get a second chance to make a first impression, so I decided to go big on the date. The stretch Lexus limousine left her breathless. I could see it in her eyes. She ain't think a thug like me was built like that.

Guess she was used to dealing with nothing ass brothers who lacked swag and style.

My suit must have impressed her too. The smile never left her face. She looked stunning in a shimmering brown silk dress that left her back and shoulders exposed. Probably Yves Saint Laurent or some other well-known designer; everything about Tocarra spoke classy. Her small feet were snuggled deep in some expensive Louboutin stiletto heels. She definitely had more ass than I first estimated. Tocarra was fine as fuck! Red carpet ready for real.

Dinner was lovely. Plenty of intelligent conversation and relevant dialogue flowed easy between us. I kept it one hundred with her and explained that I was a thug through and through. I thought that might scare her off, or make her fall back, but instead she seemed more intrigued.

"Are you a wanted man?" she asked in a sexy voice and used the stirrer to play with the ice in her drink. Her hazel colored eyes danced with fire as she flashed a beautiful mega-watt smile. I didn't want to expose too much of my thug to her too soon, so I answered in a way that matched her flirtation.

"I don't know. You tell me, Tocarra. Am I a wanted man?" I asked and smiled at her.

Our eyes locked, and we boxed for a few seconds. She shifted in her seat, giggled, and said, "Maybe not." We continued to let our eyes do the talking.

"So what do you do for a living?" she finally asked.

"Make money." I answered with a straight face.

"I mean, how do you get paid, Wahdatah?"

"By any means necessary."

"Hmm. So I see." Tocarra nodded. "Can I be totally honest?" she asked.

"Definitely."

"Everything about you is a big turn on for me," she admitted. "I don't know what it is, but something about you excites me. You kinda remind me of one of the characters in my books."

"How is that?"

"I'll let you read about him. Then you tell me what you think." She confessed that on more than one occasion she had fantasized about being with a thug. I was trying to make her fantasy come true . . .

After dinner, we took a stroll along the sandy shore of the Pacific Ocean. The stars and a full moon was our backdrop as we walked hand in hand and just took it all in. While we talked we touched on serious subject matter that brought out the more passionate and emotional side of one another.

"So tell me, Wahdatah, what is the one thing that you want most in your life?" she asked.

I looked out over the huge body of water next to us and gave her question some serious consideration. It was the first time a woman had asked me a question like that at a moment like this. I was drawn to her even more because of it.

"The one thing that I want most in life?" I repeated while I searched for the answer.

"Um hmm." She squeezed my hand harder and leaned her body against mine. Tocarra was getting more and more comfortable with me, and I was diggin' that.

"The one thing that I want most in my life is to have a family. To me, a family consists of a good woman who I can wife, some kids, and a solid foundation to build it on because that's something that I never really had growing up." I felt her hand let go of mine, but I kept holding onto hers. At that moment something about her body language changed. "You okay?" I asked, looking at her.

She looked away and said, "Yeah, I'm fine." I sensed that she wasn't being truthful, but I let it go. Whatever was bothering her would eventually come out, so I changed the subject.

"Tell me more about yourself, Tocarra." I stopped and pulled her close to me. The water licked at our toes as we stood near the ocean's end.

"Ask me more about myself," she replied, pushing her softness up against me.

"Where were you born?"

"Baltimore, Maryland."

"Is that right? What made you come to California?" I asked. My hands caressed her arms until goose bumps formed on them, and I pulled her even closer; her hair tickled my nostrils. She smelled like jasmine and pomegranates.

"I had a scholarship at San Diego State. I ran track and played basketball."

"So you're competitive. I like that," I told her. "What happened to your track career?"

"Tore my leg up runnin' in a championship meet. That was the end of my athletic career."

"Sorry to hear that."

"It's okay. Thanks to my injury I discovered my passion for writing. During my rehab I had a lot of downtime, so I wrote to pass the time, and it eventually became my first love."

"That's what's up. Take a negative and turn it into a positive."

"Yup, that's my motto." She pulled back and looked up at me. "What's your motto?"

" . . . I don't know." I shrugged. "Never really thought about it." Her question made me question myself, but I didn't want to think that much so I flipped the subject. "So what about your parents? Do you have any brothers or sisters?"

"You're deflecting, but it's cool. My parents still live in Baltimore, and no, I'm an only child." Tocarra left home at age sixteen after her parents split, and her mother's new boyfriend had abused her. That was a lot to take in on a first date. There wasn't much I could say after that.

Again, the water lapped at our toes. We stood silent in each other's arms, lost in our own thoughts looking across the never-ending body of water. The light from the moon danced across the water's surface. The next wave of water washed over our feet and wet our ankles.

"What do you want to be in life?" she finally asked, placing the left side of her face flat against my chest.

"Alive and living on my own terms. And you?"

"Happy. I just want to be happy." She nestled closer to me, and we stayed like that for a while.

Eventually, we turned and walked further up the shore where the sand was dry. When we stopped, I turned and cupped her chin with my hand.

"This is the most interesting time that I've ever had with a woman on a first date," I told Tocarra.

"Yes, it has definitely been a good first date."

She had been through a lot and yet she still persevered. I liked that she was about solutions not problems. Her style was fly, and she held my interest outside of the physical. It was our first date, but I already knew that I wanted her around more. I felt like she would challenge me rather than just chill with me. She had something I wanted and she didn't even know it; stability.

We looked into each other's eyes and smiled. Before I knew it, we shared our first kiss. Her sweet tasting tongue sought after mine, slowly at first, kinda tentative and unsure. But immediately we found ourselves trying our damnedest to swallow one another's mouth.

Her silk-clad ass cheeks felt right in my hands. I could hear her moan with approval several times when my piece poked up against her stomach. When her hand gripped it, I felt her body go limp against mine. I broke the hot, passionate kiss.

"I wanna—"

"Shhhh." She put a finger against my lips and sank to her knees. In seconds she had my joint out and in her hand. Tocarra looked at my brick hard dick and whispered to it. It sounded like she was speaking French. She kissed the head and then slowly sucked my entire shaft into her mouth. The head of my dick hit the back of her throat; her bottom lip touched my nut sack. The knuckles in my toes cracked and dug into the soft sand. Her head game was ridiculous! All nine inches was buried in her hot, wet mouth, while her tongue rolled around doing impossible shit all over my dick.

When she pulled back, and the cool night air hit my exposed meat, I shook and shut my eyes. I could tell Tocarra truly took pleasure in sucking on a dick. At times she feasted on my swipe like she was starving. Then she took her time and slowly devoured the dick with so much sensuality, I almost lost it on more than one occasion. I opened my eyes and took extreme pleasure in the scenic beauty of the moment—getting some bomb head on the beach at midnight, looking up at the moon and the stars. *First dates don't get no better than this!*

Quite a few minutes passed while Tocarra did her thing. Then, as suddenly as she started, she stopped. She rose up and whispered against my lips, "Take me home and fuck the shit out of me, Wahdatah. Fuck me like you mad at me!" Her sudden flip to freakier mode made my dick harder than a baseball bat! *I'ma pound her ass out so viciously, she ain't gone know how to act after I'm done with it!*

I took her home and dug into that pussy like I was deep sea oil drilling. I fucked her in every position I could think of, and a few she thought of as well. We sexed all over her beautiful home.

After nutting in her twice and bringing her to three body-jarring orgasms, we stretched out in front of the fireplace twisted up like a pretzel. Her head rested on my chest while we chopped it up near the crackling fire. I could feel her breath against my skin.

"Earlier when I asked what you did for a living you seemed reluctant to talk about it. You just said that you make money. Are you a drug dealer, Wah?"

I wasn't offended by her asking what I did for a living, but I didn't feel like I knew her well enough to tell her the whole truth about how I got my paper. At the same time I didn't want to start a relationship off with a lie. I paused for a minute and contemplated on how to answer her question. "Nah, I ain't no drug dealer, but I do my thang. You feel me? I'm a gangsta, and I do what I do. That's how I get mines." I shrugged.

An uncomfortable silence followed my answer. After several seconds she spoke. "Have you ever killed anyone, Wah?"

I had killed before and knew I probably would kill again, but for some reason her line of questioning was pissing me off. I took a deep breath thinking of a way to put an end to her interrogation.

I guess she grew tired of my delayed response. "Well, have you?" she persisted.

My face frowned into an angry mask. Her pestering was irritating the fuck outta me. "What's with all the questions about my get-down? You act like you the fuckin' police or something!" It came out a little harder than I meant, but it was out there now. So it is what it is.

"I was just asking a fucking question, Wah, trying to get to know you better. Obviously it's some shit about you that you're either ashamed of, or you're uncomfortable with. Don't make your problems my problems!" She pushed herself away from me and sat up. Then she brought her knees up to her chin and closed her arms around them. A temper tantrum.

Shit!

At first I wanted to apologize, but then I plexed up. *I guess the truth really does hurt.* I stood up and started to get dressed. "I'm outta here. I ain't with all this bullshit. You gettin' at me like you the po-po or some shit." I wanted to tell her that she was right, but my pride wouldn't allow me to. I snatched up my phone and turned to leave.

"So, that's it? This is how it ends, Wahdatah? You walkin' out like a coward because you're afraid to tell me the truth about who you are or about what you do?"

Her words stopped me in my tracks. Her tone was icy. I could tell she was mad, possibly hurt even. If I didn't like her I would've slapped her ass for calling me a coward. I took my hand off the doorknob and turned. "You better check yourself about how you gettin' at me. You got me fucked up—ain't no coward over here." Our eyes locked and I mean mugged her ass.

"Then prove it. Sit down and tell me about the real Wahdatah Mitchell."

I looked at her like she was stupid. "Yeah, right. Whatever, Tocarra. I told you more than enough about who I am! I'm out." I slammed the door behind me. Then I walked toward the Charger wondering if I had just fucked off a good thing. I liked Tocarra a lot, but I didn't like the fact that she kept pressing me about my get-down.

If it was meant to be she'll holla back. She has my number.

DEEPLY ROOTED

CHAPTER FIVE
Gunplay and Gangsta Shit

Baby Shug

The trio of thugs sat in the small motel room facing each other with mean-mugs and angry expressions. On the bed between the three gangstas sat six kilos of cocaine and a backpack full of big faces. The tension in the air had become so thick you could reach out and touch it.

"What part of the game is this, potna!" Baby Shug angrily directed his question at the men who now stood on the opposite side of the bed, stiff and tense.

"This the part of the game where shit happens, nigga! And when it happens you gotta be ready for it and do what you gotta do. The fact that you sittin' up in this bitch by yourself with no security is the shit that happened, and me and the homie here deciding to take both the dope and the money is the 'what we gotta do' part of that equation. But don't trip, Baby Shug. When I pump these slugs in yo' forehead you ain't even gon' feel it, bruh. At least I'm being considerate before I bang this heater on yo' ass, you dig?" the taller of the two said. His hand loosely clutched the pistol dangling near his pants pocket. Having the upper hand seemed to give him a boost of confidence.

"I knew you two ma'fuckas couldn't be trusted. That's why I had a plan B for your bitch asses," Baby Shug spat back.

DEEPLY ROOTED

Thoop!

Before anyone could speak, the taller of the two fell forward on the bed. His head half torn off from the shot that blasted through the window. The bullet ripped through the thin curtain and exploded the instant it pierced his skull.

"Oh shit! What the—" Before the shorter of the two shady thugs could finish speaking on it, Baby Shug touched the trigger on his 9-millimeter and sent two shots into his chest. His body slumped against the wall, lifeless and unmoving. Baby Shug calmly tucked the 9-millimeter back into his waistband. He had anticipated the shorter shady thug being off balance once his partner's head burst open. He had all the confidence in the world that his right hand man, Camron, would execute the game plan perfectly. It's what made the two of them the most feared up and coming gangstas in San Diego.

Only a year ago the two young Crip goons were in the streets smashing hard, moving half and whole ounces to line their pockets and maintain their lifestyles. Today, the deadly duo was playing with bricks and rubbing shoulders with higher caliber cats whose names were making noise in the streets.

Their rise was fast and furious, their methods bold and brutal. They had high expectations and huge aspirations. The two young goons took pleasure in gunplay and gangsta shit.

Camron burst through the motel room door brimming with excitement and awash with animation. "One shot ursky on that bitch ass fool, homie. What! What tha fuck you know 'bout that, cuz!" he exclaimed exuberantly after stepping over the body of the taller thug, who now lay sprawled out on the dingy rust colored carpet looking a twisted mess.

He slapped hands hard with Baby Shug in celebratory fashion before taking in the grisly scene.

"No doubt." Baby Shug wore a big smile on his face when he backed up off the embrace. "Homie, I wasn't even finished sayin' the words 'plan B' when ol' boy's head exploded, and his bitch ass tipped over a done deal!"

The two street savages quickly went about tossing the bricks inside the gym bag and snatching up the backpack of money the two thugs had brought with them.

"Make sure you cover up that brick he cut open when he tasted that shit. Ain't no sense in wastin' none of that good raw, homie. I want er' nickel worth. You feel me?" Baby Shug told Camron, before he walked over to the tall thug and rifled through his pockets.

"Don't trip. I'm on that, cuz," Camron replied. He looked up and saw Baby Shug tearin' off the dead thug's pockets in search of more money and other valuables.

"What the fuck is you doin', nigga?" Camron asked.

"Bruh, I just told you I want er' nickel worth. I ain't bullshittin'! I want all mines, cuz!" he shot back with a wicked grin and a sinister gleam.

"Wow, is there no honor amongst thieves anymore?" Camron clowned with his tag team murder partner.

They dragged the two lifeless bodies to the shower and piled them one on top of the other.

Some minutes later, Baby Shug slid behind the wheel of the 2012 baby blue Escalade and leaned back into the soft leather. He twisted the ignition and pushed a button, and the luxury big boy whip instantly turned into a Young Dro concert. The speakers throbbed violently with that extra bass. He reached into the stash box and extracted a fat blunt, and then sparked the tip up and puffed until it was fully engaged. He held the potent smoke in as long as his lungs would allow, before exhaling and doing it again. In a matter of minutes, the bomb trees, aptly named 'Trainwreck', crashed into his mental and had his mind stuck on float. Baby Shug passed the blunt to Camron and yanked out his cellphone.

"Hey you! What's up, daddy?" his thug missus, Miko, answered in a soft voice.

"What's good, Miko? Ay, check it out. Me and Cam on our way over, so be ready for us and make sure it ain't no traffic at the spot, ai'ight?" he instructed her.

"Okay, fa' sho', boo. I'm here by myself now. Did everything go all right?" she asked, her voice full of concern.

"I'll holla at you when I get there, but don't trip. We good, ma. You feel me?"

"I feel you, daddy. I love you."

"I love you too." He ended the call.

Baby Shug whipped the Escalade through the Southeast streets and blowed the bomb bud in his cockpit while Young Dro spit out slapper after slapper on that Best Thang Smokin' CD. The Escalade was pushing through the streets like a heavyweight champion.

Twenty minutes later, Baby Shug parked the 'Lac truck next to Miko's gun metal gray Acura. They exited the car and headed toward the house with hands on pistols, eyes on everything else.

"You think we should get rid of the sniper rifle since it got another body on it?" Camron asked before twisting the doorknob.

"Yeah, it don't make no sense leavin' no evidence around that could get us twenty-five wit' a kickstand," Baby Shug told him and walked into the living room. "Besides, I got a Mac-90 wit' the 50 round clip, silencer, infrared beam, and night vision lens on it. We can use that on our next get-down. Remind me to hit up Big Bolo from 47 Block and see if he got any more of that elite ass firepower he be slangin'."

"Okay. Tell Miko er'thang is in the backseat." Camron was referring to the gun used to kill the tall, shady thug at the hotel.

"Fo' sho'." Shug dropped the bag on the sectional sofa. "Miko!" he hollered out.

"Yeah, baby, what's good?" The Puerto-Rican and Creole goddess hugged her dude and kissed him passionately.

"Take the Escalade and get rid of er'thang in the backseat. Here." He handed her the car keys. "And go put this in our spot." He walked over to the backpack full of bricks.

"Okay. After that, do you want me to pick up some take-out? Or do you guys want something home cooked?" Her voice was like soft music. Her body was exquisitely designed: 36D-24-38. Her skin, the color of coffee with a teaspoon of milk poured in it. Long, silky, dark hair that reached the middle of her back where her waist narrowed and her backside flared dramatically, showcasing her round bubble ass. "I'ma swoop Monisha up on my way back too, okay Cam?"

"Ai'ight, do that, and take-out is cool," Camron responded.

After Miko bounced, the two confident Crip criminals sat down and relaxed with Hennessy filled glasses while sharing a blunt amidst a continuous roar of laughter. Thug music and kush smoke filled the air.

Camron leaned back and blew out more smoke. "Have you thought about what direction you wanna go in next, Shug?"

Shug swallowed some Hennessy and sighed. "Yeah. Actually, I have. I think it's about time we start regulating the dope game, and sew up the entire Westside, cuz."

"That's what I'm talkin' 'bout! I'm witchu' all the way on that. Who you thinkin' about puttin' on the team?" Camron was by no means weak, but ever since they were kids he almost always deferred to Shug, who was by nature an alpha male. Camron felt comfortable playing the backup role. His shooting skills were second to none; he knew Shug heavily relied on him for his murder game.

"I'm thinkin' about puttin' the big homie Boscoe on and lettin' him make his pockets fatter."

Camron cut his eyes at Baby Shug. Boscoe and Camron weren't the best of friends. They were homies from the same set, but they didn't get along. It had been that way ever since Camron knocked Boscoe for his girl, Monisha, the woman who was currently Camron's better half. Although Shug had mad love for him, Camron felt absolutely nothing for the nigga.

ICE MIKE

"I know y'all ain't the best of friends, cuz. But Boscoe is a killa too, and I trust him. If we gonna lockdown the Westside then I need people around me who I can trust— people who'll kill for me without hesitation."

What he said made sense. Camron would go for it, for the time being.

DEEPLY ROOTED

CHAPTER SIX
Bad Vibes and Bad News

Wahdatah

My phone was buzzing like crazy in my front pocket.

"Hello?"

"Hey, baby. How you doin'?" She greeted me in a near whisper, not her normally jovial tone.

"Oh, hey Granny. Long time no hear from. What's wrong? Is everything okay?" I immediately got a bad vibe when I heard my grandmother's voice.

"I need you to come by the house, Wahddy. I'm afraid I have some bad news about your father."

"That nigga ain't my father, Granny!" I banged on her out of anger.

"Watch your mouth with me, Wahddy. Don't you dare disrespect your father like that!" Her tone made me check myself. I loved and adored my granny, no matter how hood my lifestyle was. No matter how much I hated my pops.

"My bad, Granny, but you know how I feel about him. He ain't never been no father to me."

"He tried, Wahddy, and that is worth something." She knew this conversation was going nowhere, as it usually did. "I need to see you as soon as possible, baby." The tone in her voice softened and seemed laced with desperation now.

"I'll be over in a little bit, okay?" I didn't know what was going on with my father, but obviously it wasn't good news.

I ended that call and started another.

"What's good, bruh?" my right hand man Drape answered.

"'I'm finna go check on somethin' tonight, bruh. I think I found the perfect spot to put our stash until you come up off that house arrest." The idea was forming as I spoke.

"Good shit, Wah. Is er'thang cool witchu' tho'?"

"Absolutely, Drape. I had some bomb ass pussy last night. I'm worth a million ma'fuckin' bucks, and I'm a free Black man finna do big thangs. So hell yeah, er'thang is cool wit' me!"

"That's what's up, Wah. Hit me later, but not too late. I got that bitch Carmelita slidin' through later tonight. I'ma crush that bitch cakes and twist her thick ass the fuck out!"

"You really need to step ya game up, Drape. That 'ho Carmelita is a straight scrape, bruh. Er'body strokin' that." I was telling him the truth. That 'ho was hella grimy.

"That scrape got some bomb ass pussy though, bruh. I be diggin' that big ole Buffy ass out like it's the bizness!" He was laughing when he said it.

"That big booty ain't worth catchin' HIV. Check your shit after you poke that, Drape. She be fuckin' with too many dudes."

We chopped it up for a while about the diamonds before I bounced. In a matter of minutes I was at my granny's house with the briefcase full of bling and my fo'-five full of bullets.

After Granny and I hugged and exchanged pleasantries, she got straight to the matter at hand.

"Baby, your daddy died two weeks ago. I went up there to visit him before he passed on, and he asked me to give you this." She held out an envelope in her wrinkled hand.

The news of his death did nothing to me. I guess it took Granny two weeks to figure out a way to tell me that my father, her son, a man she knew I couldn't care less about had died. He'd *been dead* as far as I was concerned. She held the envelope out there in front of me adamantly, while I stared at it like it was a piece of shit on her hand. I hated my father with a passion, because he wasn't there for me growing up. My childhood was hard, and I blamed him for every foul thang that ever happened in my life. I couldn't describe the feelings I'd felt for him for the past twenty-three years. To mentally go back to that place, my childhood, would be catastrophic to my current state of happiness. I closed my eyes. *Fuck that fool He never wrote me! He never called me! He never did a ma'fuckin' thing for me! I hate that ma'fucka!* Thoughts of my past flashed across the back of my eyelids and forced me to relive the pain. An angry tear dropped from my eye. My jaw muscles clenched, and I swallowed hard.

"Take it, baby. It might have the answers to some of the questions that you so desperately sought after while growing up." She was hugging me tight now, like she used to do when I was a kid. It helped soothe the pain. Her hug made so many bad memories disappear, temporarily. I took the envelope from her hand and stuffed it into my back pocket.

"I'll be in the backyard, Granny. I need to be alone so I can clear my mind and figure out some things."

"Okay, baby. I'm right here if you need to talk. Make sure you say goodbye before you leave, Wahdatah."

"Ai'ight, I will."

I went to the backyard through the garage. On my way, I grabbed the old shovel that had been hanging on the wall since I was a kid. I stepped into the cool night air, adjusted my fo'-five, shifted my fitted hat, and turned it. I looked around the backyard and thought how little it had changed. It had been my sanctuary, the place I went to get a peace of mind when I was troubled with strife. It was the spot I relied on to restore my sanity when I felt like life was driving me crazy, for real. I don't know what it was about that particular part of the backyard that I was so drawn to, but ever since I was around six or seven years old, I would find myself retreating to the backyard under the big lemon tree near the fence. The leafy canopy and the shade it offered had often sheltered me from the hot sun or cold wind. I used the huge dirt mound under it as a chair, my personal dirt packed La-Z-Boy. It was my quiet space, my therapeutic refuge.

After a couple hours of some me time, I would always come away from it with a refreshed mind and a reinvigorated spirit. My granny respected my space and never disturbed me when I came out here to chill up under the lemon tree. She understood this was how I worked shit out within. It was how I untwisted the tangled webs my world seemed to weave around me.

Deeply rooted under the lemon tree was the place I felt most comfortable hiding the briefcase full of diamonds and jewelry. With shovel in hand, I set the briefcase on top of the dirt mound and started digging. As I tossed dirt aside, I thought about the fat Mafioso Joey Cheese and wondered if the diamond deal would go as smooth as I hoped it would.

Joey Cheese was a shady ma'fucka who definitely required watching. But he was the only person I knew who had the kind of paper I wanted for the bling I had. As I dug the hole deeper, my gut was telling me something. I couldn't put my finger on it, but a fucked up feeling settled in the pit of my stomach warning me not to trust Joey Cheese's fat ass.

DEEPLY ROOTED

CHAPTER SEVEN
Motivation

Wicked

Wicked pushed the white Cutlass through traffic while his thoughts wandered aimlessly from one roguish possibility to another. Being fresh out the penitentiary without a job, or any viable work skills put him at a disadvantage, and made it more difficult to even entertain any serious thoughts of searching for a job. That very thought process fostered a strong hope that the words his old cellie had spoken held some truth to them. *What if that old bastard really did have five million dollars buried somewhere under a lemon tree?* That question and the possible answer to it spurred him on. It motivated him to think that his life would be so much easier if he were rich. The possibility of a shortcut to ridiculous riches was something that held his hopes hostage. Something about the way Bad Boy had said it when he said it stuck with Wicked. The look in Ol' School's eyes and the honesty in his voice, although desperate, was something that resonated with him.

"I need to settle this shit once and for all!" Wicked declared with finality over the Young Jeezy track that throbbed through the speakers of the Cutlass. His mind was made up; he was going to find out one way or another whether his old cellie was indeed an unfortunate millionaire, or a lying ass delusional clown.

DEEPLY ROOTED

The Cutlass came to rest at a stoplight. The bass filled beat seemed to shake and rattle the body of the white on white whip. Wicked fired up a blunt and took two strong tokes. The blue-gray smoke clouded up the cockpit of the hooptie. He reached over and set the kush stick in the ashtray. When he sat back up, a powder blue '64 Chevy slid up next to him.

His peripheral summarized each image: top down, two deep, in all blue. Automatically, Wicked's hand dipped down to his lap and gripped the pug nose .44. *Never can be too careful in these Southeast streets*, he thought.

The rapper Scarface could be heard threatening somebody on some gangsta shit, even though his windows were rolled up and Young Jeezy was still spitting about thug motivation.

The occupants of both vehicles made eye contact. Wicked clutched the pug nose .44 tightly and caressed the trigger lightly.

"What up, nigga? Fuck you lookin' at, cuz!" the brown-skinned Crip who sat in the passenger seat said with animated anger. He snarled, exposing his gold grill. The sun beamed, and his grill glistened in the sunlight just like the twenty-four-inch gold rims.

The low rider's front half rose up slowly and froze. Then the back half followed suit. The ass dropped low, stopped, and the front end bounced hard a couple times before the tricked-out whip locked up high up off the street.

Wicked mugged the two Crips and began to lift the pistol off his lap, preparing to shoot through the window of his car.

Both Crips in the powder blue low rider simultaneously sensed that gunplay was at hand. As one, they reached for their heat. The passenger, a chrome .38 pistol. The driver, a black Tech-9. The music in both vehicles was loud; the turnt up tension between the rival gang members was even louder.

Wicked clenched his jaw muscles and zoned out everything around him. His fist wrapped tighter around the pug nose, and it seemed his heart beat in rhythm to the Young Jeezy track thumping hard and fast through the speakers.

The two Crips held their respective straps in a death grip. This was the type of gangsta shit they were confronted with on a daily in The Southeast Planet.

Shots were about to be fired! Somebody was finna die!

Wheeeeeeehhww! A police's car siren screamed its loud arrival on the scene.

A traffic violation was being served and carried out across the street. There would be no gunplay today, at least not for now.

The light turned green.

Wicked looked over at the two Crips and made eye contact. He mouthed the words 'fuck you', and then pushed the Cutlass into the flow of traffic, satisfied with the aggravated masks the two thugs now sported.

The two Crip gangstas, King and Nico, stewed in anger but relaxed after the white Cutlass pulled off. King dropped the low rider to the ground and the Impala effortlessly floated down Imperial Avenue.

Blocks away from the near fatal incident at the intersection of Euclid and Imperial, the Four Corners of

Death, Wicked eased up to the curb and parked in front of an address he had come to remember well. The only address printed on any of the envelopes for his cellie. . It was Bad Boy's mother's house.

Knock . . . Knock . . . Knock . . .

The door opened slowly, and a soft voice spoke from behind the black metal screen door.

"Hello, how may I help you, young man?" Granny asked with cautious concern in her voice. Her presence was shielded behind the dark wrought iron heavy screen door.

"Um, yeah. My name is Joseph Thomas, and I was a friend of Bad Boy's—I mean Marquis Mitchell. He was my cellie at Calipatria for a coupla years. Actually, I lived with him for the past two years before he passed away. I got to know him pretty well while we were cellies, and I promised myself that when I got out I would stop by his mother's house to check up on her and see if she was okay. Her name is Mary Mitchell, and I was hoping that I could talk to her about my time spent with her son." Wicked intentionally softened up his voice and spoke with proper grammar. He wanted to come across as an intelligent, concerned friend of a deceased buddy, not the murderous thug that he truly was.

Born and raised in Southeast San Diego, Mary Mitchell was all too familiar with the iniquitous Southeast mentality. She adjusted her grip on the nickel plated .25 pistol she held behind her back before she responded to the stranger.

"That's so kind of you. I really do appreciate your thoughtfulness." Her position relaxed slightly at the mention of her recently deceased son. Bad Boy had been her only child, and a big part of her desperately wanted to know more about her son's final days. She normally would've dismissed the notion of even entertaining some stranger knocking at her door, but it was the compassion in the unfamiliar man's voice that put her fears and suspicions at ease. Granny was eager to know more about her son. "I am Marquis' mother. My name is Mary Mitchell." She tucked the deuce-five in the top of the stocking under her flimsy cotton dress before she unlatched the lock on the screen door and opened it slightly. Then she pushed the heavy black iron door open and invited Wicked in. She had no idea of the evil presence she had just allowed into her domicile. "Please, come in and have a seat. Make yourself comfortable."

Wicked delicately took her dainty outstretched hand and shook it gingerly before taking a seat on the black leather sofa.

Forgetting her manners, Mary Mitchell immediately inquired about her son. Wicked patiently told her about their relationship, the father/son like bond they had formed while living in the 9 x 12- feet concrete cage.

He told her of the letters he had written for Bad Boy when his health had become so deteriorated that he couldn't perform the most simplest of tasks, such as writing. He was able to convince her, and win her over once he revealed specific details that only a person very close to her son would know. She had become completely engrossed with Wicked. Ten minutes into the conversation, and after several curious questions and painful answers, Mary Mitchell found her manners and remembered her hospitality.

"Please excuse me for being so rude," she said, feeling somewhat embarrassed. Granny rose from her seat. "Can I offer you something to drink, young man?"

"Uh, oh no. I'm good, thank you." Wicked respectfully declined the offer. "Call me Joseph, please." He was doing his damnedest to sound and act like a regular, ordinary reformed black man.

"Are you sure? I make the best lemonade in California, freshly squeezed lemons from the lemon tree right outside in the backyard."

At the mention of the words 'lemon tree', Wicked's ears tingled like a climax. His heart rate accelerated, and the hair on his arms and neck stood straight up. His curiosity had become more than aroused. It was overwhelmed by an insatiable hunger to know more. That hunger needed to be fed now!

"Lemonade, you say?"

"Yes, I make a delicious lemonade. Sweet with a touch of tartness that literally tickles the taste buds." Granny giggled softly, proud of her homemade lemonade.

"In that case, Miss Mary, I accept your gracious offer. How could I resist such a delightful temptation?" Wicked fully committed to his role of innocent, square black man.

"I'll be back in a couple of minutes then."

With that, Granny disappeared into the kitchen. This allowed Wicked the opportunity to stand up and stretch. He peeked out the window to catch a glimpse of the lemon tree, hoping it would yield some sign that it indeed possessed vast riches that would make his life unimaginably divine. He touched the pug nose pistol in his waistband and thought for the briefest of moments to pull it out and bust on the old lady. Kill her right now and take his time checking for the hidden treasure under the lemon tree. Those thoughts vanished as suddenly as they had surfaced when Granny reappeared holding a tray with two tall glasses brimming with freshly squeezed lemonade and a pitcher holding more lemonade with slices of lemons and ice cubes in it.

"Here you go, young man—excuse me, I mean Joseph. I hope you enjoy it." Wicked took one of the glasses and brought it to his lips. He sipped tentatively at first, then guzzled most of the tall glass down, savoring the delicious taste of the sweet, tart drink that had a delightful twang to it.

"Yes, this is definitely the best lemonade I've ever had the pleasure of tasting."

Granny gushed with glee. "Why thank you, Joseph. You are so kind."

The young thug had had enough of playing house with the old broad. He made up his mind that he would bounce now and come back another time under the cover of darkness to do some further investigating. To put to rest once and for all the mystery of whether there was really a shit load of scrilla up under the lemon tree.

Wicked made fake conversation for a few more minutes before finally coming up with an excuse to leave. Five minutes later he was pushing the Cutlass through the light late afternoon traffic with millionaire daydreams moving around in his mind. He stopped by a Home Depot and purchased a flashlight, a shovel, and a duffle bag. He headed back to Jracia's crib with two thoughts provoking his pleasure: five million tax-free dollars and that good, tight, wet pussy between Jracia's thick yellow thighs.

The lemon tree in the backyard kept popping up in his mind. Wicked could barely wait to return.

DEEPLY ROOTED

CHAPTER EIGHT
Lifelong Enemies

Wahdatah

I can't lie. A thug like me was definitely digging Tocarra's style, so squashing our petty beef came easy. She called and said, "May I speak to the sexy, intelligent man with the tatted up frame that looks chiseled from granite?"

The moment I heard her voice and the compliment, I smiled. My years of coming up through the juvenile and adult prison system had been good to me like that. Exercising and reading had my body and my mind in tip-top shape for real. All flattery aside, I fronted on her like I was still pissed. "The man you're lookin' for *may* or *may not* be here. Depends on who's asking?" Tocarra didn't need to know she had it like that.

"Tocarra Rhodes-Robinson is asking, and I'm looking for the man that not only has the chiseled body, but he also has a gorgeous smile and pretty white teeth. As a matter of fact, that same man once told me some skinny chick in his unit had the nerve to ask if he bleached his grill."

She got to me. I chuckled it up a bit and thought about my reply to the skinny chick. *Hell naw. My grill is naturally white like this.* Nah. I wasn't conceited by any stretch of the imagination, but no doubt I had every reason in the world to be confident about how I looked. Being confident was a part of my DNA. My swag was natural, you feel me?

"So what's up, Tocarra?"

"You are, Wahdatah Mitchell. I'm over our little mishap. How about you?"

"Yeah, I'm all good, ma."

"Glad to hear that. So I was just thinking we should go on a date to the movies. I'll go ahead and shower and get dressed. See you tonight at eight when you get here." She hung up before I could respond. Obviously, I wasn't the only one with confidence and a natural swag.

An hour and ten minutes later I was smelling and looking fresh and clean. Dolce and Gabbana denim, crisp white tee over a wife beater, fresh Jordan's, and a white fitted. I stuck a chunky three-carat diamond in my left earlobe and placed my favorite Rolex on my wrist. Then I snatched up the .45 Desert Eagle, my phone and keys and headed out the door.

I flexed the muscle in the Mopar Charger as I pushed the triple black whip toward Tocarra's block. Thirty-five minutes later I texted her to let her know I was turning down her street. As I pulled up to the curb in front of her crib, she was locking her front door.

Damn, she's gorgeous! Tocarra was sexy, successful, and had a body that usually only existed in wet dreams.

The Rick Ross track shook the block up when I opened the door. I made my way around the front end of the car and met her on the sidewalk. We hugged, and then shared a soft, tender kiss.

"Damn, Tocarra! You look hot as hell, ma." I twirled her around. She was off-the-chain fine! She wore a white silk charmeuse top, with low-rise jeans that beautifully cupped her ass cheeks and wrapped tightly around her legs from hips to ankles. The Jimmy Choo pumps had her height a few inches under my 6-feet 2-inches. Her skin was flawless. Those hazel eyes were mesmerizing.

"You look handsome and debonair yourself, baby," she said, looking me over.

"You rockin' the fuck outta that new hairdo." I immediately noticed she had hooked up her hair in a way that framed her face perfectly.

"Boy, stop cussin' so much." She squeezed my dimples between her thumb and fingers and kissed my lips again. "Thank you though." She touched the diamond encrusted medallion hanging on my thick platinum chain. Her fingertips traced along the diamond out cursive 'Wah'. "I like your chain. It's nice." She looked up at me and smiled.

I smiled back. "So what's good? You ready to bounce, ma?"

"Yes sir, I sure am."

"In that case, beautiful black woman, your chariot awaits you." I held the passenger door open and she got in. We were in traffic with the quickness.

I turned the music down to a whisper, and we chopped it up all the way to the movie theater. Our vibe was electric, and the conversation between us flowed naturally. Tocarra didn't seem to be caught up with any hang-ups or pretentiousness, which only added to her attractiveness. Laughing was a regular occurrence, smiles were often, and the flirting was non-stop. It was as if we had known each other for several months, not several days. We were drawn to each other. The chemistry between us was strong, but it was almost as if we were both hesitant to expose how we actually felt. We jumped into it so fast, having sex on the first date, but so far everything was a good fit. With the exception of that one argument because she asked one too many questions!

After arriving at the theater, we were just about to step to the concession stand when I heard a familiar voice speak my name. I tensed up and touched my chrome at the sound of my worst enemy's voice.

"Wahdatah-Wahdatah-Wahdatah . . . It's been a minute since I've seen you out here in the streets, nigga. What up wit' that? You stopped being a fighter and turned into a lover or some shit?"

I shifted my attention to the man I considered my nemesis since grade school. I put my hand on Tocarra's hip, and moved her behind me in the event the confrontation became physical. Our last one definitely had. I mugged him up and down as my hand inched closer to the fo'-five. "So that's how you spend your days now, Baby Shug? Checkin' for me? Is your girl here cool wit' the fact that a thug nigga like you is out in the Southeast Planet streets checkin' on other niggas?" My response made him twist up his face.

He was visibly upset and the two chicks he was with stood in an uncomfortable silence, not sure how to react to the exchange. I peeped his homeboy's hand disappear behind his back, probably touching on his steel.

"Real funny, Wah. I see you still got jokes."

"It is what it is, bruh." I didn't really have much to say to him. Our history of beefin' went way back to when we first bumped heads in juvenile hall at the tender age of eleven. He was a Crip, and I was a Blood. So off the top we were on opposite sides of the fence, but that wasn't where our beef originated. Our mutual disdain for one another was born the day after we met when both of our mothers got into a fistfight in the visiting room at the juvenile detention facility. To this day I never knew why they fought, but the fact that they did was reason enough to make us lifelong enemies.

In all, we had four fights. Our last squabble ended with me putting him on his back pockets in front of Fam Bam, an indoor swap-meet frequented by damn near all of the urban community in San Diego. The only reason Baby Shug and I never resorted to gunplay or any deadly type force is because as teenagers while doing bids in the California Youth Authority, on two separate occasions we saved each other, so-to-speak, during a couple of riots against some Mexicans. In jail, regardless of your gang affiliation, if you were in a race riot, under no circumstances could you allow a member of your own race to get jumped by another race and not help out. No matter how much you disliked one another. That was looked at as worse than being a punk.

We had both saved each other once from knife-wielding Mexicans, and for that we begrudgingly respected each other's gangsta to a point. We had an unspoken understanding that it would never be beef to the point of death, just a deep dislike for one another. A profound disdain for one another that was deeply rooted. I couldn't stand him, and I knew he couldn't stand me.

We stood there in the concession stand line mean-mugging each other for a few tense seconds until I grew tired of the stare down. I got our snacks, grabbed Tocarra's hand, and then pushed past him and his crew, our shoulders brushing barely.

"Whatever, nigga," I heard him say before his entourage erupted into raucous laughter.

After the movie, during the drive back to Tocarra's house she turned in her seat and said, "Can I ask you a question?"

"You just did." I clowned and smiled.

"I'm serious."

"Go ahead, what's up?" I told her.

"What was that all about with that guy back there in the theater? It seemed like there was a lot of tension between the two of you." She cupped her chin and rested her elbow on her leg waiting for my response.

"It is a lot of tension between us. Our beef goes way back to when we were kids. We don't like each other; it's as simple as that." I told her as little as I felt I had to.

"Why?"

"Why what?" I was suddenly growing annoyed. *Why she always askin' questions!*

"Why do you guys have beef?"

I sighed my impatience. "Because I'm a Blood and he's a Crip, and Bloods and Crips don't like each other. Bloods and Crips automatically beef with each other," I tried to explain to her.

She turned back in her seat, and we drove in silence for a few blocks listening to the music before she started with the questions again.

"When we were in line and you guys faced off, I noticed your hand inching closer to your gun. Would you have used it?" Tocarra asked.

I frowned and gripped the steering wheel tighter. "Tocarra, why you ask so many weird ass questions?"

"What! Ain't that a bitch!" She scrunched up her face. "Why do you get so damn insecure when I ask questions? Hold up . . . or is that a weird ass question too?" She rolled her eyes and folded her arms. Then she sat as far away from me as she could.

I felt bad for getting at her like that. "My bad, Tocarra. I apologize."

She didn't respond, but maintained her position, damn near hugging the passenger side door.

"I said I was sorry." I tried to clean it up. "What. You ain't got nothin' to say to me now?"

She turned and flashed her mean face after I said that. "Yeah, I got something to say to you, Wah. Take me home!"

DEEPLY ROOTED

CHAPTER NINE
Under The Lemon Tree and Deeply Rooted

Wicked

*A*in't nothing like good pussy before stealing five million dollars, Wicked thought. He needed something to do to kill the time until the sun went down. He had a trunk full of digging gear and as soon as it was dark enough and the old lady was asleep, he planned on hopping her fence and getting up under that lemon tree. He was gonna be leaving Mary Mitchell's property either the angriest person on earth, empty-handed, or the happiest man alive and five million dollars richer.

His thoughts were rudely interrupted when out the corner of his eyes something caught his attention. As he drove leaning low in the white bucket leather seat, he caught a glimpse of the same powder blue '64 Chevy Impala low rider that had eased up next to him at the Four Corners of Death and stunted on him. The memory of the two Crips trying to hoo-bang on him at the intersection was still fresh in his mind, and it left a sour taste in his mouth. Had it not been for the po-po showing up on the scene unexpectedly, there was no doubt in his mind that somebody would have been clacked out the game.

Looking at the low rider sitting in front of the burger joint, Wicked was again struck with that familiar feeling. Somebody was finna die today.

Within minutes, Wicked eased into the burger joint's parking lot without the Crip sensing his presence. He watched the street thug known as King thumbing through a thick wad of big faces trying to impress the light-skinned chick with the fat ass leaning on the table, giving him all of her attention. When King peeled off a couple and extended his hand to the pretty, slim sistah, Wicked knew he had been given an opening.

"That should cover my order and leave you with a nice lil' something to play with," King said as he picked up his bags and prepared to shake the spot.

Before the woman could take the two big faces from his hand, the loud thunderous explosion from the pug nose .44 sent a warm sensation spraying the girl's face. Burnt hair and gunpowder scented the air. She looked up to see a nearly headless King standing stiff. His body was propped up against the same table she had just so seductively been leaning over. Before the scream could escape her fear-filled chest, her tongue involuntarily slithered out and lapped at the warm noodle-like substance that splashed her face. She spat the brain matter out like poisonous Top Ramen noodles, and let out an ear-piercing scream that would have put to shame any white girl in any scary movie.

The Crip's body eventually fell over with a thud across the middle of the tabletop. In doing so, it gave her a clear and frightening look at one of the most notorious Bloods in Southeast San Diego.

Wicked mugged the screaming woman with a look of pure evil as he raised the pug nose thumper up and pulled the trigger. As far as he was concerned, she was a witness, and as loud as she was screaming, no doubt her voice worked perfectly fine. He couldn't let her words be the reason he went back to the penitentiary for the rest of his life.

Doom! Doom!

He hit her with two in the left titty and toppled her over. He picked up the wad of big faces and relieved the Crip called King of his expensive jewelry. "You ain't gonna be needin' none of this where you going, Blood," Wicked said as he casually left the scene of the bloody double homicide.

Wicked walked past the powder blue low rider and popped off a couple more shots that punched holes in the TV monitor embedded in the dashboard and the headrest. He jumped in the Cutlass and left the scene in such a nonchalant manner that it even unnerved a few of the thugs who had witnessed the cold-blooded walk-by.

Figuring that the Cutlass would be hot now, his first order of business was to make it disappear and get a fresh whip. Jracia's black Camry would have to do.

After putting the thick, high yellow freak to bed with a good dose of some daydream dick, he was dressed in all black with the digging tools in the Camry's trunk. It was eleven o'clock at night, and chances were, Granny would be knocked out with slumber when he parked three doors down from her house.

Wicked was slow and careful with his approach, mindful not to arouse any suspicion, or attract the unwanted attention of a nosy neighbor. A dog a few yards away started barking. A block over, a car horn wailed out its impatience. He looked around one final time to make sure the coast was clear, and to see if it was all good for him to go do his dirty. Climbing the fence with the shovel in one hand and the pug nose .44 in the other, was a job in and of itself. He landed softly on the grass and tiptoed to the lemon tree. Once there, he knew he'd run the risk of exposing his presence by hitting the flashlight and illuminating the ground under the tree. A couple of loose lemons had fallen from the tree. He kicked them out of the way and saw what looked to be a huge mound of dirt. *That could definitely be a spot with five million dollars under it.*

Just as he was about to turn the flashlight off and mark his spot by shoving the shovel into the dirt, he saw a freshly dug up patch of space to his left. His face twisted with curiosity. Upon closer inspection, there was no doubt in his mind that the ground there had been dug up recently. His heart rate accelerated. Sweat broke out on his brow, and he wiped at it with the back of his gloved hand. Wicked moved his tongue around the inside of his mouth in an attempt to generate moisture. His mouth had suddenly become bone dry. He set the flashlight on the ground, no longer caring about a nosy neighbor. The shovel stabbed into the ground, and he tossed the dirt that came up with it over his shoulder. The shovel stabbed into the ground again.

Pop! Pop! Pop!

A gunshot, quickly followed by two more gunshots exploded into the dark night and frightened the fuck out of him. He palmed the pug nose and ran as fast as he could in the direction he had come from.

Pop! Pop!

Two more shots sounded off, only this time he heard the bullets crash into the wooden fence in front of him. The sound of wood disintegrating on contact made it all too clear to Wicked that his life was in grave danger. He reached behind him with the .44 and busted off a couple shots.

Doom! Doom!

Glass shattered behind him somewhere. A woman could be heard swearing.

Wicked hit the wood fence at a full sprint and flipped over the top of it. He landed on his feet but lost his balance. His head bapped the green meter box on the wall of the building next door. He fell to his knees.

Pop! Pop! Pop!

The fall might've saved his life. All three bullets smacked into the stucco two feet above his head.

"Lemme catch yo' ass snoopin' around here again, you son of a bitch, and I bet I don't miss yo' ass next time!" Mary Mitchell's voice was loud and clear in the dark night.

Pop!

One more shot into the fence for good measure. Wicked flew down the block in the black Camry, lights out, foot mashing on the gas, and his heart pounding like a Swizz Beats track. *Who the fuck was that and how the fuck did they know I was back there?* The thought raced wildly through his mind as he tried to catch his breath. He angrily slammed his fist against the steering wheel and started thinking of another way to get up under the lemon tree.

DEEPLY ROOTED

CHAPTER TEN
The Letter

Wahdatah

I just had to shoot at somebody, Wahddy—"
I didn't let her finish her statement. "Say no more, Granny. I'm on my way." I ended the call, tossed my cell phone on the front seat, and broke every traffic law possible on my way to my grandmother's crib.

"Are you okay?" were the first words out of my mouth once I got there.

"Yes, I'm fine, Wahddy. A little shook up, but Betsy here had my back." She held the .25 pistol up with pride.

"Tell me what happened. Start from the beginning and take your time, Granny. Try to remember as much as you can." I was preparing myself to hear her tell me some shit like somebody was trying to break in her house or something. I knew my granny stayed strapped, so I wasn't surprised about that revelation. She was my grandmother, true, but Granny was Southeast San Diego born and raised. She understood the Southeast mentality well. "I heard a noise out in the backyard."

When she said the word 'backyard' I broke into a full all-out sprint, hurdled the sofa, and one-hopped the coffee table. I was in the backyard in about five steps. I bee lined straight over to the lemon tree. My heart got stuck in my throat when I saw a shovel near the buried briefcase. I can't express the kind of relief I felt wash over me when I realized that whoever it was that breached my granny's property never got the chance to finish the job.

She followed me to the backyard. I listened to Granny tell me about how she heard a noise that woke her up from her sleep. She shook it off and chalked it up to her imagination. When she heard another noise, she went to the window with her pistol in hand and saw the light in the backyard under the lemon tree. She described her pistol play as I dug for my briefcase. I pulled the dirty diamond filled briefcase free.

"What is that, Wahdatah Mitchell? And why the hell is it in my backyard?"

"It's something that is important to me, Granny. Don't trip." She stared into my eyes hard. "I just put it there the other day. I don't know how somebody found out about it."

"Don't you be bringing no dope up in my house, Wahddy. You know I don't play that shit."

"It ain't no dope, Granny. I promise. Besides, technically, I didn't bring it *in* your house either." I smiled and winked at her.

"Don't play with me, boy! What the hell is it?" she asked, trying to mean mug me.

We looked at each other for a minute before I winked and smiled at her again. She didn't return my smile. "Whatever it is, take it with you. I don't want it at my house."

Then she hit me with a bombshell. "Reminds me of the night before your father went to jail. You weren't born at the time, Wahdatah, but he was up all night in this damn backyard digging and digging and digging. Right there where that packed dirt mound is at. The next day he got into some trouble and ended up killing a man. When I went down to the county jail to see him, he made me promise to leave it alone and never talk about it again, and to never let my curiosity get the best of me. You know how I am about keeping my promises, Wahddy."

"Hold up, hold up, hold up, Granny. What are you telling me?"

"I-I'm. Didn't you read the letter I gave you? Before your father died he said the letter would answer a lot of the questions you may have had growing up."

"What!"

"Didn't you read the letter?"

"I gotta bounce, Granny!" I kissed her cheek and broke wide.

With the briefcase in the passenger seat and the chrome in my lap, I hightailed it straight to Drape's pad. The letter was still in the same back pocket I had stuffed it in the other night when I went to dig the hole for the diamonds. I wondered what type of secrets that letter held from my father's past. I guess I'd find out once I got home. But right now I was on my way to see what was good with Drape.

I stomped on the gas and pushed the Mopar Charger through traffic like a mad man. In minutes I was at Drape's spot, mad as fuck and ready to murk something! I jumped out, stuffed the chrome in my waist, and walked with the briefcase in my left hand.

I couldn't keep walking with all this bling in my possession. Obviously, somebody knew about the jewelry. They also knew I hid the briefcase in my granny's backyard, and the only person who even knew I had the jewelry was Drape.

Also, Drape was the only one who knew I went to hide it somewhere. *And why the fuck was my father diggin' up the backyard the day before he went to prison for killing a man?*

Knock, knock, knock.

I waited in front of the wood door with the briefcase at my side, and my hand inconspicuously holding the fo'-five.

"Who is it?" a female with attitude asked from behind the door.

For a minute I thought about throwing two or three hollow tips through the door. "It's Wahdatah! *Open* the door."

I heard the chain unhook and the lock unlock. The door opened, and I mobbed into the living room. "Where Drape at?" I turned and asked.

"What, you can't say hi to a bitch?" Carmella's nasty ass tried to sound sexy and flirt with me. The shady bitch had the nerve to openly lust on a ma'fucka with her eyes. She licked her juicy lips and winked at me.

"Bitch, get the fuck outta my face with that shit!" I mushed her forehead and pushed her backward. When her body contacted the arm of the sofa, she lost her balance and fell back onto the couch, T-shirt slid up, feet in the air, and pussy exposed in her small ass panties. The look on her face would've murdered me if looks could kill.

"Why the fuck you do that shit, Wahdatah? Nigga, you ain't shit! You think you all that but you ain't—"

I silenced her when I pointed the Desert Eagle at her ass. "Shut the fuck up 'fore I pistol whip you, bitch, for disrespectin' me."

She paused like a DVD and looked like a nasty ass black mannequin. I left her there looking stupid and walked to the back room. The door was closed.

Tap. Tap. Tap.

I stood to the side and tapped the tip of the fo'-five softly against the bedroom door and waited for him to open it up.

"It's open, nigga. Come on in," Drape yelled from somewhere far back in the room.

Is he on the other side of the door with a thumper ready to bust on my ass or what? Does he know that I suspect him of some slick shit? Am I paranoid now that I got all this jewelry? Am I puttin' a ten or a two? My mind was running wild with mad questions. *Fuck it, he just gone have to clack on me!* I thought, pumping myself up. I used my foot to push the door open and stepped in slowly with the chrome up.

"What up, Wah? Fuck is you trippin' on?" He was sitting on the bed in his boxers and a wife beater, twisting up blunts. He looked up at me, and then quickly went back to doing his thing.

"Drape, this nigga Wah pushed me and knocked me on my ass for no reason!" Carmelita barged into the room and tried to put some shit in the game. She ain't know she was fucking with an angry ass goon nigga though. Now was not the time to be playing with a ticking time bomb. I was finna teach the rat-ass bitch a lesson she would never forget.

"Bitch, put ya ma'fuckin' hands up in the air!" I drew down on her like I was back in the jewelry store all over again on my goon shit. The Desert Eagle was pointed at her face as I stepped closer. In two steps the chrome touched her teeth. "I said put ya hands in the air before I blow a hole in yo' ass, bitch!" I whispered. I was so close to her, my warm breath made her blink. She put her arms up and started crying. Her eyes darted over to Drape, desperately begging for his help. The look on her face was hella comical! When she saw he wouldn't be coming to her aid, her body shook so hard it looked like she was pop-locking. She shivered like she was freezing.

"Take off that shirt and tear them fuckin' panties off, bitch!" I ordered with the hand-canon still parting her lips. She stepped out of her stanky underwear with the quickness. "Now walk yo' tough talkin' ass over there to the fuckin' window!" My voice was cold and cruel, gun steady in my hand. She knew I wasn't bullshitting.

Naked, Carmelita looked out the window with uncut fear painted all over her face. I pulled the glass back and opened the window wide. No screen. Two stories up. Cold night air made her nipples stiffen and her areola bumped up from the chill.

"Please don't do this to me, Wah!" Her tough-talking ass was bitching up now.

"Close yo' mouth, 'ho, and climb yo' ass up there. Get up there and jump, bitch! Jump to ya death!" The fo'-five kissed the nape of her neck. She trembled fiercely, and then sobbed uncontrollably.

"Please, Wah. I'm sorry. Don't do this to me, please! I swear I was just playing. I didn't mean no harm! I promise I won't get at you like that no more!" She was halfway out the window, asshole naked and crying like a baby.

Drape put the purple on pause and watched with amusement while I dogged her ass. I was about to make her jump out the window, and he was just sitting there taking it all in like a ghetto movie.

Carmelita looked down to the alley below her and held onto the window with her left hand and the wall with her right hand while her naked ass squatted on the windowsill. Scared to death.

"Bitch, the next time you disrespect me like that, I swear I'ma make yo' funky ass dive head first into one of them beer bottles down there in that alley. You hear me, 'ho?"

She nodded emphatically.

"Now get yo' punk ass down, bitch!" I stepped back and inwardly laughed at her scandalous ass. This was the second time Carmelita tried to get at me like that in the homie's house. I told her punk ass last time not to disrespect my gangsta. Testing my friendship and loyalty was a slap in the face, and I wasn't the type to take disrespect lightly.

She jumped back into the bedroom and ran straight to the bathroom. *Probably in there releasing her bowels.*

"What's good, bruh?" I turned to Drape and threw the briefcase on the bed. The chrome was still in my hand. I wanted to see the look on his face and gauge his reaction when I mentioned the incident at Granny's house.

"Ain't nothin', homie. Finna blow one and lean back for a while. I just piss tested, so I'm good to go. You feel me?"

I looked at him and waited for him to make eye contact.

"Somebody tried to steal the briefcase from my hiding spot, Drape. They almost got away with it too."

"What! How the—what the fuck happened, Wah!" He spilled the loose weed and the rolled up blunts onto the floor in the process of jumping to his feet.

I tucked the chrome in my hip. His reaction convinced me that he wasn't the one in my granny's backyard. Then it dawned on me: *he still got that ankle monitor on, so it ain't no way he could've left his house.* But still, I wasn't trusting anybody. It ain't no telling who was in the backyard digging up under the lemon tree. Trust was non-existent right about now. So until I found out who the hell was in my grandmother's backyard, everybody was suspect and subject to being shot.

I heard the front door slam shut. Carmelita was getting the fuck away from me as fast as possible.

"Why you clown that bitch like that, Wah? You know she might not ever slide back through this way again. That's some good ass pussy right there that you ran off."

"Fuck that 'ho! She disrespected me." He could tell I wasn't trying to talk about that shit, so he left it alone.

We chopped it up about the incident at my granny's, and then discussed how we should holler at Joey Cheese's fat ass. He was the connect, the one who was gonna take the diamonds up off us and put a million dollars in our pockets. At that moment, Joey Cheese was the one person who could put a million dollars on the table in one whop.

Drape didn't know Joey Cheese all that well. Outside a couple of very brief encounters when we did jobs for the fat mobster in the past, he never really had any contact with him. At least not to my knowledge.

Now that all of that was handled, I needed to get back to my crib and see about that letter. *What the fuck did my father have his hands in way back in the day? What was so important that it was worth spending the rest of his life in prison?*

DEEPLY ROOTED

Part II

DEEPLY ROOTED

CHAPTER ELEVEN
Step Ya Game Up

Shug

His eyes devoured her curvaceous frame. The juices of desire pooled under his tongue while thoughts of what he wanted to do to her ran wild through his mind. Shug wrapped up the phone conversation as soon as he saw Miko step into the bedroom. Dressed in a black silk and lace panty and bra ensemble that had her flawless banging body poking out in all the right places, the beautiful sex-kitten now had his undivided attention. Her perfume floated across the room and teased his sense of smell. Miko struck a sexy pose, so he could take in all of her sensuous beauty.

His excitement was obvious, evident by the huge bulge near the opening of his boxers. His love muscle tried to free itself from the constricting silk fabric. He could see her thick, dark nipples pushing against her bra, desperately begging for his attention.

"Come here, ma. Let daddy get a closer look at you."

Six long-legged steps later, she was in his arms. Her softness pressed hotly against his hardness. When he kissed her he tasted the cherry flavor on her tongue. She closed her eyes and savored the masculine scent of the Armani Code cologne. The way he effortlessly handled her body with strength and confidence while he teased her mouth with the most impassioned tongue kiss made her pussy flow with delight. She could feel her excitement puddle up with her creaminess. She loved his thuggish lovin'.

Before she realized what happened, he had unhooked the clasp to her bra and her tits sprang free. His fingers were soon twisting and pulling on her hard nipples. Miko moaned in his mouth when he pinched them with just enough force to send an electrical surge down her spinal column, through the crack of her ass, and deep into the wet split between her legs. Sensing her vulnerability to his manipulations, he pulled his tongue from her mouth and immediately dipped his head low until one of her nipples was in his mouth.

"Oooh!" A soft moan escaped her parted lips.

He sucked. Licked. Softly bit. Sucked again. Then he softly blew cool air onto her erect bud. Her body shook with pleasure. Goose bumps covered her skin, and she melted in his arms. Miko found herself searching frantically for the hole in the front of his boxers. She squeezed his thickness and pulled on his length with one hand. The other hand held the back of his head to her breast, ensuring that his oral attention stayed right there.

His fingers released the other nipple, and the palm of his large hand slowly trailed down her flat stomach. He grabbed a fistful of her panty and gently pulled upward, causing the silk and lace to dig up between her swollen wet lips. His tongue on her nipple grew more aggressive. The material wedged deep between her lips, rubbed against her clit and made her body shudder. She threw her head back in ecstasy and grunted with pleasure.

He knew then that she was more than ready. Shug pulled the soaked silk from between her lips, and in one fluid motion, palmed her ass and picked her up. She wrapped her legs around his waist and slowly sank down onto his elongated manhood until his thickness was buried to the hilt in her hot, sticky wetness. The lone thought that kept flashing through her mind was how deep his dick seemed to be up in her. With his mouth torturing her titty with pleasure and his thug meat filling her happiness up, Miko began to roll her hips and ride his dick slowly, lustfully. She fucked on his dick until her pussy exploded with excitement, her juices drenching his meat thoroughly.

Shug felt her creamy wetness dripping onto his heavy nut sack. He let her nipple go, and instantly her mouth found his. Her tempo sped up as she bucked faster. When she felt her second orgasm approaching, she bounced harder, biting his bottom lip, loving the pleasurable pain that kept punching her in the center of her essence. No words, only grunts and groans of sexual gratification as she repeatedly impaled herself on his thug pole. A spasm racked her body, and wave after wave of pleasure washed over her until the feeling overwhelmed her; she flooded his dick with more of her cum. Shug put her down on the bed and without any need for further direction, Miko was on her hands and knees doggie style, wanting it bad.

Twenty minutes later, Shug was still deep-stroking the pussy, almost in slow motion. His pleasure-pounding, hitting her pussy with indescribable joy. Miko begged him to fuck her harder. Faster. Deeper. He refused to give in to her pleas, preferring to tease her soft, wet, sensitive spot without mercy. His slow-stroke continued to drive her crazy with lust, his pace never wavering. When she tried to throw the pussy back at him, he controlled her movements with his strong hands on her hips. Only when he felt her pussy tighten up and constrict, then explode from her third orgasm, did his stroke switch up. He plowed deep in her pussy, fast, hard, body jarring strokes. Her pussy began poppin' with joy as her hot, wet hole slushed and slurped with the sounds of satisfaction. His open hand slapped her ass cheek hella hard, just as his dick head hit the bottom of her heart, it seemed.

"Yes, Shug! Oooh yesss! Right there, hit it right ma'fuckin' there, baby!" He had her exactly where he wanted her.

He reached around and rubbed her clit roughly with the surface of his fingers as he pounded her out from the back. Miko thought that her third orgasm would never stop; at least she hoped it wouldn't. She came longer and harder than she had ever cum before. She felt his hot nut splash deep inside her pussy, and her body shook one final time before the two of them fell into a heap of contentment on the bed.

"Damn, baby, that shit was the bomb!" he whispered into her ear, and then nibbled on her earlobe as they lay in bed together breathing heavily.

"Yes it was, daddy. That deep stroke ain't no joke. That shit is the bizness!" She laughed and kissed him passionately on his lips, then his chin, and finally on his neck.

Miko grabbed the remote and turned the music down to a whisper. She snuggled up close to him with her face on his chest, his heart beating in her ear.

"Can I ask you a question, baby?" Her soft voice was warm against his skin.

"Of course, ma. What's up?"

"How long do you plan on fuckin' around in the streets?"

Baby Shug hesitated, not quite sure of her question.

"Whatchu' mean, Miko? I don't understand what you tryin' to ask me, baby. I mean, is you tired of fuckin' wit' a gangsta or somethin'?"

"Never that, Shug. I was raised up in the thug life, remember?" She took hold of his limp penis and started squeezing his joint as her tongue licked across his chest. Miko smiled inwardly when his dick jumped to life in her hand. Her pussy wet back up at the thought of another round, knowing that he would try to kill it the second time around.

"Then why you stressin' me 'bout bein' in the streets?"

"I ain't stressin' you about bein' in the streets, baby. As a matter of fact, I want you to be in the streets. What I'm stressin' you about is how you got yourself out there in the streets. I'm stressing you about bein' in the streets on some regular type shit."

"Fuck is you talkin' about, Miko?" He was more confused now than when she first started with this line of questioning. She ruffled a couple of his feathers with it too.

"What I'm talkin' about, baby, is when are you going to stop playin' in those streets and step your game up? Get up out them streets and get on some boss shit?"

"Step my game up? Some boss shit? Is you serious, Miko! I be out there in them streets on some beast shit. Ma'fuckas know Baby Shug ain't the one to be toyed with!" His retort was wrapped with anger and 'I'll-be-damnededness'.

"Yeah. Step your game up, daddy. When I look at you, baby, I see a boss. You and Camron be out there in them streets taking life and death chances for a little bit of weight here and there, a little bit of dough here and there. Your life ain't worth just a little bit of weight, or a little bit of dough. So why do you risk it for a little bit of weight or dough? No disrespect, baby, but I think you need to take your worker hat off and put your boss hat on. For real. Step ya' game up and get it like a boss is supposed to get it." These feelings had been hidden away in her heart for months now. She felt like now was the perfect time to speak on it.

Her words cut a little bit and left him momentarily at a loss for words. It forced him to take a serious look at his approach to the game. They stayed up late into the new morning chopping it up and ping-ponging thoughts and sharing ideas with each other as they had on so many other occasions. It was times like this that made him truly appreciate her being five years his senior. Her outlook on life was refreshing in a thuggish type of way, and it always made him challenge himself to go bigger. Miko had a thug nigga mentality.

She reminisced and told him stories about her father and his crew. When it was all said and done, Miko had vividly painted a clear picture of her once legendary father and his team of moneymakers. She pulled out her photo album and showed him old pictures of her father, who had been killed when she was just a five-year-old girl. His death had crushed her to the point where she had to be hospitalized in a mental health facility for a short period of time. Her father's death killed something inside of her. It murdered her humanity.

The pictures she showed Shug were of a handsome, thuggish looking man who bore a striking resemblance to her. A tall, light-skinned gangsta with long, good hair. The kingpin in the photo stood proudly in front of stacks of money piled waist high. His arms stretched out wide, basking in the rich glory of his gangsta.

The picture of hood wealth was beyond impressive to Baby Shug. It gave him a goal to aim for. He definitely didn't want to be anything like his deadbeat father, a man he looked at as being an old, washed up, has-been who was sitting up in the penitentiary. He never knew his pops. His moms made sure of that. He never wanted to know him either. As far as he was concerned, he hated the man he had never met, the man who had never so much as written him a letter. All Baby Shug knew about his father was that he was a wanna-be thug back in the day. That, and the rumors that it was because of his father that his mother had been murdered.

Shug trusted Miko more than he trusted anyone in his world. She was his saving grace, the woman who had introduced him to the meaning of true love. They had met by chance, but to him it was destiny.

He had just dropped off a friend when they bumped into each other outside an apartment complex. They clicked instantly and had been together ever since. Everything about Miko was high-class gangstress. He had never met a chick who was so hood in her understanding of the game and so intelligent when it came to everything else in life. She was the one chick he could depend on; she had always been there for him in his time of need. He knew she would one day be wifey and the mother of his kids.

Baby Shug fell asleep against her titty with thoughts of how good her pussy felt. In minutes he was snoring loudly, dead to the world. Miko slowly slid from up under him and quietly crept to her phone after hearing it vibrate on the bedside table. She looked over at Shug to make sure he was knocked out when she spoke. "Hey, Cream, what's up with it?" she answered in a conspiratorial whisper.

"Same shit different toilet, Miko," the masculine voice with the rich baritone responded. "Can you talk right now?"

Miko peeked at Shug's back again before tiptoeing out of the room to finish her conversation.

CHAPTER TWELVE
A Father's Secrets

Wahdatah

I parked the car against the curb and carefully looked over the outside area for any signs of an intruder. Although I rested my head here, I couldn't be too careful after the shit that went down at Granny's house. I eased out the muscle whip and put security on the Mopar Charger. Then I checked the walkway leading up to the front door for footprints. None.

With the fo'-five close to my hip and pointed straight ahead, I was prepared to bust if a bush rustled or a branch so much as cracked under the foot of somebody laying in wait, ready to murk my ass. My senses were on high alert. Every part of me was on edge now. I took the same precautions after I stepped inside and closed the door behind me.

Satisfied that no one had violated the privacy of my home, I was able to relax a lil' bit. My first order of business was to grab a bottle and a glass. I splashed some Hennessy in the short glass and tossed it back. The wet fire that burned a trail down my throat loosened me up a taste and took the edge off. The Desert Eagle never left my hand as I went about my routine of taking my jewelry and coat off and tossing it on the sectional sofa. Then I checked my mail, turned some music on, and kept it low. After I kicked off my shoes, I put my phone, wallet, and keys in the crystal dish on the table.

It didn't take long for me to remember where I last put the letter. Actually, I'd never taken it out of my back pocket after Granny gave it to me. I had gotten so caught up with digging the hole for the briefcase that I completely forgot about it. I walked over to the dirty clothes hamper and pulled the pants out.

What the fuck is this letter? My father's secrets were sealed inside the envelope. I inhaled before I tore it open, took the folded paper out, and held it. For a minute, I just sat there looking at it, not knowing what to expect. Suddenly, an unexpected rush of emotion came over me. This was the first time my father had ever written me a letter, or tried to contact me in any way, shape, or form. I was twenty-three years old, and I had never so much as spoken a word to my father. I hated his ass so much it hurt! Yet, as I held his letter in my hand I felt compassion for the man I had detested all of my life. I breathed out my apprehension and unfolded the paper.

To My Son Wahdatah,

If you are reading this letter that means that my time on this earth has come and gone. I know that nothing I say can undo the pain that you had to endure growing up as a child without a father in your life, especially after your mother was murdered. But I hope that after reading this letter you will better understand why I did, or didn't do so many things over the past twenty-three years.

I want to first start by apologizing to you both for not being the father that you wanted, needed, and deserved to have . . . But I had my reasons, and right or wrong, I had to live with the consequences of my actions.

When I was 18 years old, I was a young and foolish small time hoodlum with two kids on the way. Yes, you heard me right, two kids on the way. You have a brother out there somewhere, Wahdatah. To be more specific, I had two women pregnant at the same time. They hated each other with a passion and probably hated me even more for putting them in that predicament. But like I said, I was an 18 year old young, foolish thug with two kids on the way, so I took it upon myself to make a bold move, a move that I thought would make me financially secure for the rest of my life, and your lives' as well. Thing is, it didn't quite turn out the way I expected it to. I killed a man the next day. A man named Kiko Dunbar. He was a big time drug dealer that I used to work for. I knew that trying to contact my kids or their mothers would be seriously putting you all in harm's way because of the connections.

The reason that I'm reaching out to you now is because I was recently diagnosed with terminal cancer, and my days on this earth are numbered. Don't be upset with your grandmother, because she didn't know much about the dirt I used to do, nor was she familiar with much of my past activities. I made her promise me that she would never pry into my affairs, and you know how that woman is about keeping her word.

I didn't have much contact with her, because I feared for her safety as well, but she wrote to me often, and kept me updated on how you were doing. She told me that you loved to sit up under the lemon tree whenever you were troubled. I'm not surprised; it was also my favorite spot as well. There was a time that it used to be all flat ground under that lemon tree, but after I made that big move that I mentioned earlier, I left a little something buried there. I always hoped that one day I would get out and be able to enjoy the fruit of my labor with my kids. But as the years passed, it became clear to me that that just wasn't going to be happening, so I decided to do the next best thing and leave all of my worldly possessions with my two sons.

Your brother's name is Marcellus Braxton, and his mother refused to give him our last name, and she did everything in her power to keep him away from my mother. But I was able to find out a few things about him over the years. I don't know his address, but he goes by the nickname Baby Shug. I don't know if you know him or not, but find him and introduce him to your grandmother. After that, the two of you should go dig up under the lemon tree. I left something there for the both of you. Hopefully, you will split it down the middle and share it 50/50 like brothers are supposed to do.

I hope the two of you will take care of each other and look out for one another. I want you to know that although I was never there for the two of you, both of you were always here with me. I've always loved you two. I loved you guys so much that I had to make the most difficult decision in my life, which was to let you go. But as hard as it was, it was either that, or lose the both of you just like I lost my baby mamas. I am sorry, son, but I had to do what I had to do. And you two are still alive, so it was the right thing to do in my eyes. I know this letter won't erase the pain of your past, or make up for what I took away from you. I just wanted to provide you with answers to some of the questions that I'm sure you had growing up. Hopefully, what I left behind will ease some of the pain that I caused. Use what I left you guys and live your life to the fullest with it. I love my sons, and I always have. Know this if you don't know anything else.

Love Always,
You're Father

Marquis Mitchell
Aka Bad Boy

P.S. Just so you know . . .
It wasn't worth it to me, son. If I had to do it all over again I wouldn't have made that bold move. I'd rather be a broke man raising kids, instead of a dying man in prison knowing that I failed you both.

I can't even begin to put into words what I was feeling after finishing the letter. For several minutes I shook my head and reread some of the bombs he dropped on me. My heart threatened to burst with shock a couple of times. Discombobulated was an understatement!

Some of the shit he was speaking on was preposterous! *Impossible!* I started hyperventilating, and had to quickstep my way to the bathroom and stick my head in the sink. Cold water didn't do a damn thing to calm my frazzled nerves. *Baby Shug my brother! My mom's killed because of some shit that my father did!* All of this shit was too much for my mind to process sober. I twisted a blunt and drank straight from the bottle until my mind was numb.

Hell ma'fuckin' naw!

DEEPLY ROOTED

I read the letter several times to see if I had overlooked something. Maybe I misunderstood something he wrote. The shit my father was talking in that letter fucked up my high. I jumped in the shower and tried to wash away the confounding pandemonium that had me staggering around the house in a mental fog.

Late into the night I lay in bed still trying to make sense of it all. I called Granny a couple of times, but she wasn't picking up. That only added to the chaos going on in my head.

I called Drape and woke him up. I needed to find a way to reach out and contact Baby Shug. My nemesis. My lifelong enemy. My brother.

While I waited for Drape to pick up, puzzle pieces from the past began to fit in and make sense. The day I received the news my mother had been shot in the face by a complete stranger when she went to answer a knock at the door was etched into my memory forever. Where I was at. Who I was with. And what I was doing when I got the news had been the back drop to my misery for years. Nobody seemed to know anything. Her death was still a cold case. I was thirteen when it happened, and it still fucked me up when I thought of my mother.

"Hello?" A sleepy voice shook me from the tragic twilight zone that I had been momentarily stuck in.

"Drape. This is Wah. I need a favor, bruh!"

"A favor!" he repeated incredulously before going on. "It's 3:08 in the fuckin' mornin', blood! What kind of shit is this? It can't wait 'til the sun come up!" His anger at being woke up in the wee hours of the morning was evident. But I didn't give a fuck about none of that.

"Naw, Drape. It can't wait. Otherwise, I woulda called you when the sun came up!" The agitation in my voice was evident too.

"Fuck type of favor you talkin' about, Wah?" He must have sensed that something was wrong, but that didn't make him any less angry.

"'Don't that bitch Carmelita fuck with that nigga Camron's girl?"

"What!"

"Carmelita! Don't she fuck with the bitch that Camron be kickin' it with?"

"Are you fuckin' serious, Wah? You woke me up to ask me that?"

"It's hella important, Drape. Real talk, homie. I need to get in touch with that fool Baby Shug—"

Before I could finish, he interrupted me. It wasn't a secret to any of my folks that Baby Shug and I had been beefing for years. Something must have clicked in his mind. If I was looking for Baby Shug like this, then something had to be hella wrong.

"What's wrong? Is everything good, Wah?" He sounded wide-awake now.

"It's a long story, Drape. I'ma fill you in later. Right now I need to holla at ol' boy though."

"Hold up. Let me hit you back in a few minutes, okay?"

"Ai'ight. Do that . . ."

Ten minutes later, he texted me Baby Shug's phone number and told me to come see him later. It took a few minutes to gather myself, my thoughts. Then I called the man who had been my enemy since childhood. My brother, if what my father said was true.

CHAPTER THIRTEEN
Rich Expectations

Wicked

W icked jerked down hard on the gearshift angrily and parked the Camry down the block a ways. He walked to Mary Mitchell's house with purposeful steps in every stride with his fists balled up, gritting his teeth. Dawn was slowly breaking the day wide open with a gloomy gray light as the sun woke up somewhere on the other side of the world.

Traffic was scarce. The soft, cold wind hit his face with a chill that made him dip his head low and push a little faster. Wicked combatted the crisp morning with a thick black hoodie, gloves, black jeans, boots, and a goon mask under the hoodie that camouflaged as a beanie. He was about to try his luck again with the fence in the back when the newspaper in front of the door caught his attention and lit his brain up with an idea.

The thick line of bushes that ran along the front of the house provided him with proper concealment. Wicked squatted low in the bushes and patiently waited in the cut for his opportunity to strike. His quick thinking was rewarded, when ten minutes later the front door cracked open. The heavy, black iron screen soon followed, and Granny appeared on the porch. The older woman gathered up the worn terry cloth robe and stepped out into the chilly morning to collect her paper.

"Oohh, it's so cold out here." She rubbed her palms together frantically trying to generate heat. When she bent to scoop the plastic-wrapped newspaper, she heard a noise and then her head exploded with pain. Her body fell over hard onto the pavement and started shaking. The vicious punch to her temple rendered the elderly woman unconscious.

Wicked looked around nervously and then dragged Granny into the house on her back. A solitaire worn gray slipper left behind, the only sign of the quick but violent encounter that had just taken place.

Five minutes later, Granny stirred from the fist-forced slumber when the glass of cold water drenched her wig and face. Wicked took extreme pleasure in her fearful reaction to seeing his face. "Yeah, bitch, it's me again. Only this time I ain't playin' nice. You understand?"

Her face twisted with confusion, the woozy cloud of knockout fogged her mind. "Who? What?"

"Shut the fuck up! Don't waste my time askin' no dumb ass questions, old bitch. I'ma give you this one opportunity to tell me the truth. If you lie to me, old lady, I swear I'ma break yo jaw. Ya heard me?" Wicked cracked the knuckles on his gloved fists.

Granny twisted her body and struggled against the restraints that bound her to the chair. She tried to be tough about it and stare the young thug down, but the look of savagery on his face soon made her rethink that strategy. She turned her head away in fear, realizing her captor was pure evil.

He grabbed her wig and twisted it in his fist until her face turned up. Her face was a mask of fear and pain. "I want to know what the fuck is up under that lemon tree out there." His words were spoken slowly through clenched teeth, like he was angrily talking to a child.

At the mention of the lemon tree, Mary Mitchell immediately came to a clearer state of mind. Off top, it dawned on her that it must've been her son's ex-cellmate who had been creeping around in the backyard the other night. His visit out of nowhere just before that made her realize that his presence wasn't a coincidence at all. This man plotted and planned the whole thing. The friendly visit, and him acting as if he was paying respects to a deceased friend's mother was all a bunch of bullshit.

The briefcase Wahdatah had dug up! All of the digging the night before her son Marquis went to prison! Filled with a renewed sense of courage, she made her mind up right then and there that no matter what this man did to her, there was no way on earth that she was gonna reveal any information to him. She'd rather die before putting Wahdatah in harm's way. Before she broke the promise she had long ago made to her now dead son, she would rather join him in heaven.

Granny coughed up a throat full of mucus, spat a thick loogy, and watched it land on Wicked's face. The thick green snot slowly rolled down his cheek. Her position was clear.

Wicked wiped the spit off his face. He bit his bottom lip and socked Granny in the jaw with all the force he could muster. A loud crunching sound followed. The chair tipped over, and Granny's head hit the floor hard with a thump. Grunting angrily, he pummeled her face and head with punishing blows that swelled her up like she had been beaten with a sledge hammer. The entire left side of

DEEPLY ROOTED

Granny's face caved in, in an ugly way. The violent punches put her back to sleep and woke her back up more than once. Then her frail body convulsed with seizures. He stood over her body and admired his handiwork with an evil smile on his face.

Wicked was beyond giving a fuck about her physical state. He went to the kitchen and returned with a large Hefty trash bag. He put the bag over her head as her entire body continued to shake. Her haggard breathing soon filled the tight space inside the plastic. After several moments her body eventually stopped shaking when death came to claim her badly beaten frame. There was no panic in Wicked. He calmly went about handling his business. This wasn't his first rodeo. He was in his comfort zone.

He wondered if the shovel he had brought with him the other night was still in the backyard under the lemon tree. He headed to that very spot full of rich expectations.

Wicked stopped short of the freshly dug up dirt. *Somebody had been digging up under the lemon tree!* Panic raced through his mind at the thought of the money not being there anymore. *What the fuck happened to it? Where the hell was it? Who the fuck dug it up? Did they get the five million?* His mind rattled off one question after another as he took in the scene before him.

Shovel . . . Fresh hole in the ground . . . His flashlight and duffle bag were still there. Something wasn't adding up. The hole in the ground was hardly big enough for a five million dollar jackpot. But as sure as he was standing there, there was a freshly dug up hole in the ground, and no sign of any money.

Fuck! Damn it!

ICE MIKE

For a split second Wicked regretted killing the old woman. Now he couldn't squeeze the information that he needed out of her. Then a thought hit him! *The money must be somewhere in the house!* He broke back to the house at a full sprint, and came to a screeching halt at the sight of Granny's body wrapped up tight and tied to the chair.

With the quickness he untied her and dragged her body out back. He started digging with the shovel until the hole was big enough to fit Mary Mitchell in it. After he stuffed her in the hole, he tossed dirt on her dead body under the lemon tree.

Wicked went back inside with intentions of searching every inch of the house until he found that five million dollars. Surely it had to be there! He vowed not to leave until he found it.

DEEPLY ROOTED

CHAPTER FOURTEEN
A Brothers' Bond

Wahdatah

For some strange reason I was a little nervous as I held the phone up to my ear waiting for somebody to pick up? *This shit is hella crazy!* I thought. The contents of my father's letter was playing tricks on my mental. I didn't know what to expect. This shit had me off-balance in a real way.

"Hello?" a gruff voice thick with sleep and agitation answered after about the tenth ring. I hesitated for a split second before I gathered myself.

"Is this Baby Shug?" I asked, knowing that it was, but trying to buy myself enough time to get my shit together.

I thought about ending the call, but that would have been hella weak. "Yeah, who the fuck is this!" His anger was uncut.

"This is Wahdatah Mitchell, bruh. I was—"

"Nigga, what the fuck is you callin' me for?" He cut me off angrily.

"I got something important that I need to holla at you about. It ain't the type of thing that I want to talk about over the phone though." I wasn't feeling the way he was getting at me, but under the circumstances I understood why he was tough talking me. I mean, me and this cat been beefin' since we were eleven. Years of feuding tended to make a ma'fucka dislike you to the extreme.

"I ain't ya homie, dude. And we ain't got nothin' to talk about. Not as far as I'm concerned."

I remained patient and maintained my composure. I was finna hit him with a bombshell, and he was probably about to flip the fuck out when I revealed it to him. One of us had to be the voice of reason though.

"Man, check this out, homie. It's not a secret that we ain't never really liked each other."

"So why the fuck is you on my phone with this bullshit then?" He cut me off again.

That made me say to hell with all this beating around the bush shit. I'ma serve it to his ass straight up.

"I just found out that we might be brothers, man! A dude named Marquis Mitchell could be our father."

Stunned silence on the other end of the line.

After a few seconds he spoke. "Whatchu' talkin' about?" His voice was void of tension.

"I'm sayin', bruh. I got this letter in my hand, and it's from my father. The shit he talkin' about in this letter is some shit that we need to talk about face to face, not over a phone." I kept the cell phone up against my ear waiting on his response, but it was quiet as hell on his end.

Did he just hang up on me? "Hello?"

"I'm still here. When you want to meet up, and where?" His voice was almost a whisper now.

"It don't even matter to me, man. You tell me where you feel most comfortable meeting at," I replied.

He paused for a few seconds before answering. "How about the IHOP at eight o'clock?"

"Which IHOP?"

"The one over there on El Cajon in East Dago."

"Eight o'clock then. I'll be there."

"Fo' sho'."

"Ai'ight then, bruh."

"Ai'ight then."

The tone of our conversation had completely flipped from hostile to humble. This was going to be some seriously weird shit. To be sitting across the table from the man I had literally been at war with for over half my life. We were going to be meeting up in a matter of hours. And I didn't have a clue how it was going to unfold. I lay back on my king-sized bed, closed my eyes, and tried to focus on what I wanted to say.

Make sure you take your pistol just in case. You never know, I reminded myself.

Two and a half hours later, I was posted up in one of the booths with my pistol on my hip. Shug walked in a couple minutes after eight o'clock. I looked at him walking toward me, and I had to admit there were a couple similarities between us.

It's a trip, because in the past I had shouted people down for telling me that. But now, sitting here in this IHOP booth after digesting and accepting my father's revelations, I was seeing things through clearer eyes.

Baby Shug strolled with a confident swagger. Baggy faded jeans, powder blue San Diego Charger throwback jersey, and a powder blue fitted hat with a pair of light blue

Timbs. I wasn't fond of the color blue, but I had to admit that Shug was making it look gangsta.

I remembered the first time I bumped into this cat. My mind flashed back to that occasion so many years ago.

Juvenile Hall . . . 2000

"Look at that lil nigga right there, Blood. He think he hella hard, homie." The homie Thun-Thun nodded toward Shug while he effortlessly dribbled the basketball between his legs.

We were in the middle of a game of one-on-one hoops to eleven points when the new kid walked into the recreation area.

"I wonder where that fool from?" I said in response, cracking my knuckles and readjusting my mean mug.

"Let's go find out about it, Wah!" Thun-Thun was always on some turnt up shit. We left the basketball bouncing on the concrete court and mobbed hard over in the direction of the new kid.

"Ay, where you from, homie?" The words were out of my mouth before I was within arm's reach.

"I'm from West Coast Rollin' 30's Crip. Why? Where you from?" The new kid's body tensed, and he balled up his fist anticipating a squabble.

"This Lincoln Park Blood Gang, nigga! What that 'B' like, Blood?" I was ready to scrap. My dukes were up, and we squared off, about to get down when one of the counselors broke through the loose circle of spectators that had begun to form at the prospect of a good fight jumping off.

ICE MIKE

"Break this shit up, y'all. It ain't going to be no fighting here today, fellas," the middle-aged counselor said in a *gruff voice. He had his whistle near his lips ready to sound the alarm for back up if we didn't follow his instructions.*

The next day our mothers got into a fistfight in the visiting room. The day after, Shug and I had the first of four fights as soon as the doors cracked open in the morning. We were eleven at the time. We stayed in juvy for six months before going to the California Youth Authority (CYA) together.

We both ended up doing a few years in CYA. I did close to three and got out when I was fourteen. I saw Baby Shug on the streets soon after. We ended up in prison together too, same yard. Thinking back on it now, our paths were so similar it was scary.

Before, I had always thought that our mothers fought because he snitched to his moms about our near fight the day before. After reading the letter from my father, now I realized they were probably fighting over him. *That's crazy!*

Baby Shug stopped short of the table just as I stood up. We mugged one another for a minute before I stuck my hand out. He left me hanging. *Probably still hot about the outcome of our last squabble*, I mused.

"What's all this shit you talkin' about us bein' brothers?"

"Here, bruh." I pulled the letter out of my pocket and tossed it on top of the table. "Read that and tell me what you think about it."

In the process of retrieving the letter, Shug's hand went up as if signaling somebody outside. I looked out toward the parking lot and scanned the premises. I ain't see nothing out of the ordinary. Maybe he saw somebody he recognized and was just saying what's up. Maybe I was just imagining shit. It was something odd about his actions though.

I sat down after he sat down and tried my damnedest not to look at his face, but found myself stealing peeks anyway. Eventually, I just said fuck it and started studying his features. I looked for signs of similarities, or anything else that would suggest we were related. *Maybe we could pass for brothers,* I finally acknowledged, just as he finished reading the letter.

"Did he really write this shit?" I could see the stunned expression etched deep into the tales of his face. His left eye twitched. His jaw clenched and unclenched while he was in deep thought. He leaned back and closed his eyes, and then let out a long breath.

"Yup, no doubt," I answered his question. "My grandmother gave it to me herself." We stared intently into each other's eyes. I was looking for reactions. He was looking for answers.

"You know it's funny, because years ago I heard this same rumor from my uncle before he went into the service, but I dismissed that shit as soon as I heard it. Lookin' back on it now, I guess I was just in denial. I didn't want to see it, because I never really liked you. Flat-out, bruh. I ain't never liked you, man."

I met his stare with a stern one of my own. "The feeling has always been mutual. I ain't never been too fond of you either."

Our eyes locked and loaded. It was then that something strong and unexplainable passed between us. As one, we both rose from our seats facing each other. I mugged him. He mugged me. Then, simultaneously huge smiles spread across our faces. We slapped hands and pulled each other close. Our embrace was genuine. The hug was sincere. Something profoundly emotional enveloped the both of us in that instance.

"Twenty-three years, man! Twenty-three years, and we spent half of it hating each other," I said in his ear.

"I know, man. Never again, bruh. We can't waste another minute of our lives beefin' with each other. No matter what type of conflict arises, we gotta stay strong, family." I could hear the determination in his voice. I could feel the resolve in his every word.

At that moment, something in our souls intertwined. The feelings in our hearts changed forever. Shug pulled out a cell phone and hit a button.

"It's good, Camron. Go ahead and bounce, cuz. We straight up in here. I'll get at you later on tonight, homie." He ended the call and stuffed his phone inside his pocket.

Right then I realized that he had his boy Camron laying in the cut, out there ready to blurk me out my boots if shit went bad between the two of us. He had been signaling somebody when he made that hand gesture before sitting down.

We spent the better part of the rest of the morning getting to know each other on a different level. Shug and I got real serious at times and spoke on some meaningful shit about our past. Why this, who that. We had a few light moments as well, where we clowned and laughed about some stuff that had gone down between us. We filled each other in on one another's history and were amazed at how similar our lives really were. Even down to the fact that our mothers had been killed on the same day, the same way. What was even more eerily ironic was that we were both in the same California Youth Authority facility when it happened, on the same yard. We were thirteen at the time and I was playing basketball; he was playing football. I remembered getting called into the office and being informed by my counselor that my mom's had been killed. I remembered it like it was yesterday, because it was the day that Shug and I had the second of four fights. It made so much more sense now. We both were angry young black boys who had suffered tremendous losses. Our parents and our hatred for each other reflected that. Our beef had been so much deeper than a Blood and Crip feud. And we never really knew what had truly fueled it. Hopefully, our newfound bond as brothers would be much deeper than our beef had been.

I may have been a Blood, and he may have been a Crip, but when we left up out of that IHOP there was no mistaking the fact that we were brothers, one from the same.

"Let's shoot over to Granny's, bruh. Y'all gon' love each other!"

"Say no more, bro. I'll follow you, ai'ight?"

"Fo' sho'. Let's roll."

With that, we were in a two-car caravan weaving in and out of traffic on our way to Granny's crib. His blue Escalade trailing the black Charger.

A brothers' bond wasn't a thing you could fake. When it was real it had a special feel to it. Like there was more than just you in this world. I had never felt anything like it.

As I stepped on the gas and pushed the muscle car through traffic, I looked up into the rearview mirror and caught a glimpse of Shug's face. *We been hatin' each other*

ICE MIKE

for years! I wonder if I'll be able to trust him. Hope he don't do nothing that force me to have to kill him.

DEEPLY ROOTED

CHAPTER FIFTEEN
Dead Man Walking

Wahdatah

*B*am! Bam! Bam! Bam!

"Granny, open up. I got a surprise for you!" I banged on the door and yelled.

"Maybe she gone, bruh. I don't see no car in the driveway," Shug pointed out, after I beat on the door several times.

"Naw, that's her burgundy Town Car right there." I pointed toward the curb. "She don't like to put it in the driveway, so she parks it on the street. So she can keep an eye on it from the front room."

"Maybe she out in the backyard then," Shug suggested.

"Yeah, that's probably where she at. Let's go."

Shug and I stepped off the porch and walked briskly toward the rear of the house. We pushed the back gate open, and instantly, I noticed the fresh mound of dirt where I had recently unearthed the briefcase. *Granny must've cleaned up after me.*

"That's the lemon tree right there." I pointed out to Shug. "It look like she was back here cleanin' up my mess."

"Huh?" Shug asked, appearing confused.

"It's a long story. I'll tell you about it later," I replied, contemplating how much I should reveal to my brother, and how soon I should do it. I wanted to trust him completely, but this was the same dude that I'd had a deep dislike toward for a number of years. Time would eventually tell if I would be able to trust him. But for right now though, I had a few trust issues.

People were known to do strange and crazy things when it came to money. On some occasions, ma'fuckas murked their own family members for the love of it. *Let's see how this play out, and then I'll know more about how much I can tell him,* I thought.

"Something ain't right, Shug. Come on," I told him while I walked. I got them butterflies in my stomach again. With my instinct on high alert, I pulled the Desert Eagle from the small of my back. Baby Shug sensed it too. He eased the Glock 9 from the shoulder holster near his heart. Together, we entered the house through the sliding glass door. *This was usually locked.* Immediately, I knew something dreadful had occurred in Granny's house.

Shug and I made eye contact. Instantly, we were on the same page. Both in murder-mode. Straps gripped tight in our hands, eyes and ears on point for the slightest noise or movement of any kind. The house was in ruins. Ransacked and flipped upside down as if a hurricane had hit it. I tilted my head in the direction of the kitchen. Shug nodded with understanding. Gun up, I slowly walked in the direction of the kitchen, ready to murder the first ma'fucka I confronted. Shug followed close behind, tiptoeing backward, keeping an eye on the rear.

"Something bad happened to Granny, bruh. I feel it in my bones," I whispered.

"I feel it too, bro. But right now we need to be on point, because it ain't no tellin' if somebody is still up in this house. And if so, how many of them are still in here?" He was whispering too.

"It's two rooms downstairs and two rooms upstairs, plus it's a bathroom on each floor. We gotta go room to room. Be careful though, because Granny could still be up in here somewhere." My voice was a pained whisper. I tried to maintain my composure, but the thought of Granny being hurt had me fucked up in the head.

After checking each room on the first floor, I motioned Shug to follow me upstairs.

As I walked into Granny's medium-sized bedroom with the Desert Eagle pointed straight ahead, everything felt wrong. *What happened, Granny?* I thought as I scanned the ransacked room before finally coming to rest on the open closet door. My eyes narrowed at the sight, and I drew in a breath. Slowly, I tiptoed toward the opening and was about to reach out to poke the clothes hanging off the wooden bar that held plastic red and white hangers. But I stopped and glanced behind me and gestured for Shug to get low and check things out. People hid under beds all the time, even though it was the most obvious spot.

Shug got on his knees with gun in hand, searching under the bed. I turned back to the closet but then stopped and closed the closet door when it suddenly occurred to me that something wasn't adding up. *If Granny isn't here, then either someone has her hostage, or they took her from here and*—I didn't even want to finish that thought. *Fuck it.* I decided to come clean to my brother. If he crossed me, I'd kill him.

I spoke to him with the gun in my hand swinging at my side. "Check this out, Shug. I had a small treasure buried in the backyard under the lemon tree. The other day, Granny called me tellin' me that somebody had been snooping around out in the backyard. So I shot over here with the quickness, thinkin' my shit had been jacked or something. But when I got here, it was exactly where I left it. There was a shovel and a flashlight near the spot where my buried treasure was, so she must've chased whoever it was off before they could get to it."

"Damn, Wah. That don't sound good."

"I know. Granny ain't been picking up her phone when I call either. She ain't here at the house, and it looks like it's been tossed the fuck up by more than one person, bruh. I don't know what the fuck is goin' on, you feel me?" A worried expression framed my face. I shook my head and fought to hold back my tears.

"Yeah, somethin' ain't adding up, homie," he offered his two cents.

"Come on, let's bounce," I told him. Shug and I left the bedroom and went back to the living room. I tried to call Granny again. This time her phone started sounding off somewhere in the front room.

"What the fuck!" I followed the sound and stood frozen with terror; Granny's phone vibrated against the table. "Somebody took Granny, bruh! She wouldn't just leave up outta the house without taking her phone. Plus her purse and keys is right there too." I pointed to the end table.

"It don't make sense, Wah. Let's go check out the backyard again," Shug suggested.

"Come on," I agreed, a feeling of fear gripped my heart.

Shug and I searched the backyard again, and were about to bounce when I was struck with a dreadful notion.

"Hold up for a minute, Shug," I told him and walked over to the dirt mound. I looked at him, perplexed.

"What's up, bruh?" Shug asked.

"When I left from here the other day, this was all dug up. But the hole that I dug here wasn't nearly this fuckin' big, bruh." I reached down for the shovel and started digging.

The fifth time I shoved the digging tool into the soft dirt it made contact with something solid. I quickly went to my knees, having an appalling premonition. Using both hands, I started digging up and throwing handfuls of dirt over my shoulder. Then my hands touched the face wrapped in plastic.

"Aw fuck!" I shouted and jumped back with shock, my mind not wanting to believe what my eyes were seeing and what my hands had just uncovered. "No! No! No! Nooo!" I cried out in pain.

Tears streamed down my face and my back shook when I sobbed my sorrow. I sat back on the heels of my feet, threw my head up to the skies, and cried harder than I'd ever cried before.

Shug knelt down to comfort me by putting his hand on my shoulder.

On more than one occasion, we had endured tragedy in our lives before, but this time it was different. It was the first time that we had to endure a tragedy together.

The image of Granny's face wrapped in a plastic trash bag crossed my mind. "Whoever did this shit to Granny is a dead man, Shug! On everything, bruh. I'ma personally gun they bitch ass down!"

DEEPLY ROOTED

CHAPTER SIXTEEN
Vantage Point

Wicked

Wicked was busy digging through a suitcase when he heard the loud banging noise coming from downstairs.

Bam! Bam! Bam! Bam! Bam!

The heavy wrought-iron door was being pounded on hella hard. He pulled out the pug nose .44 and proceeded with caution down the stairs toward the front door. With gun in hand, he peeked through the curtains and wondered if he would have to slump somebody else. And if so, would the loud bark of the .44 make one of the neighbors call the po-po?

When he looked out the window there was no one outside at the front door. *Must've left,* he thought. Wicked stuck the pistol back in his waistband and went back to searching. He took the stairs two at a time until he was inside the master bedroom, Granny's room. He rifled through her dresser drawers and flipped them onto the floor. Wicked turned the mattress upside down and looked under the bed. He was on his way over to search Granny's closet when he heard two distinct male voices entering the house. He turned to go confront the noise, prepared to empty the pug nose .44 into whoever it was, but at the last minute he thought better of it and decided against it. His vantage point didn't allow him to get a shot off without exposing himself first. Then he saw each man pull out their pistols. *It's two of them and one of me.* Wicked knew he couldn't win if he shot it out with them. He'd almost completed his search of the house for the five million dollars, and he had every intention of leaving up out of there with that loot. *I ain't leaving here without my money!* He didn't know who the two men downstairs were, and frankly, he didn't give a damn. All he knew was that there was possibly five million bucks hidden in Bad Boy's mama's house somewhere, and he needed that! That money was his as far as he was concerned. If he had to kill two more people to get it, then so be it.

While the two thugs were downstairs strategizing their sweeping search of the house, Wicked laid in the cut and soaked it all up. He listened with the attentiveness of a faithful church member to a pastor's sermon.

When the two thugs reappeared from the kitchen, Wicked stepped further back into the shadows, and observed their movements until they disappeared into one of the downstairs rooms.

Moments later, when the two men started up the stairs, Wicked ducked into Granny's closet and prepared himself for a gunfight. His sweaty palm gripped the pug nose tightly, and he concealed himself behind the many clothes that hung from the rack above his head. With the .44 aimed at the closet door, he waited quietly and slinked deeper into the closet until he was completely hidden. His breathing was measured, his focus keen. He was ready to kill a man.

Wicked was concocting evil things when a bead of sweat dripped down his brow and fell onto his hoodie. He remained as still as a statue in the back of the closet and soaked up everything that had been said. At the mention of a buried treasure Wicked's heart beat like a drum. Obviously, the one who was doing most of the talking had taken the money at some point, and then put it all back under the lemon tree, only to take it again.

He got my five million dollars! I'ma wait for they bitch asses to leave; then I'ma follow 'em and jack they ass for the loot. The pug nose in his hand was dying to blow up. Wicked's fingers caressed the curved surface of the gun, ready to explode the hand canon. *I'ma blow his ass up if he poke his head in here!* he thought.

Heavy footsteps slowly neared the closet's opening. "Come on, let's bounce," he heard the one who had been doing most of the talking say after stopping at the closet's entrance.

Wicked breathed a sigh of relief after they left and relaxed his body.

As soon as the two men went into the backyard through the sliding glass doors, Wicked crept out of the house. It was obvious to him now that the money wasn't here. One of the dudes in the backyard had the five million, but he wouldn't have it long. *That money is mines!* Wicked told himself as he made his way back to the Camry. *I'ma sit my ass out here in the cut and wait for them two fools to shake the spot, and then I'ma follow they ass, catch 'em slippin' and get what is rightfully mines!*

Wicked sat low in the Camry's front seat and waited halfway down the block. His eyes never left the front of Granny's house.

DEEPLY ROOTED

CHAPTER SEVENTEEN
Far More Sinister

Wahdatah

After digging up Granny's body with a little help from my brother, something came over me. The reality that a far more sinister thing was in play here could no longer be denied.

The other day somebody had been over here on the verge of digging up the briefcase, before Granny ran them off with her pistol. That same somebody more than likely returned and killed my grandmother and buried her in the backyard. I'm sure that same person is the one responsible for tearing up her house too. *Who could it be? How many of them were there? Is it somebody I know? How did they know about the briefcase?* All of these questions were boxing around in my brain, punching at my curiosity, swelling my thoughts up with confusion. Dazed with many questions, I staggered around for answers.

My brother was shook up too. I could see it in his mannerisms. He kept pacing back and forth, seemingly at a loss for words. He wanted to talk, but probably felt like now was a time where silence was the best form of comfort that he could offer me. I wanted to hear his thoughts though; I wanted to hear what his take was on the why, what, and who?

"Holla at me, Shug. What's on your mind, bruh?"

He stopped pacing and looked over to me. "I think we need to look at this entire thing from a realistic point of view, Wah, and see it for what it really is."

"Whatchu' talkin' 'bout, bruh? I am lookin' at it like that. This is as real as it get wit' me, nigga." An attitude crept up in my voice and revealed itself when I spoke. I was offended by him thinking that I wasn't seeing this shit for what it was.

"Naw, naw, Wahdatah. You takin' what I'm sayin' out of context, homie. I know you takin' this shit hella hard, bruh. I can only imagine your pain, family, but I ain't talkin' about it like that. What I'm sayin' is this: this is a murder scene, bruh, and our prints are all over this house. So when her body is eventually discovered, we are gonna be the prime suspects in her murder at some point in time. Real talk. This shit can end up gettin' pinned on us! I mean, stranger things have happened, and you know as well as I do that the judicial system has convicted people for a lot less, and with a lot less."

"You're right about that, Shug. I never looked at it like that. My head is so fucked up right now that I ain't thinking straight."

"What we need to do right now is straighten our hands out and make sure that we don't come up on the po-po's list of possible suspects."

"I agree witchu', my nigga." He was dead on right. As angry and as hurt as I was, I had to keep things in perspective.

I was sitting here with a dead body in my lap, and dirt from the crime scene all over me. My handprints were all over the shovel, as well as the house. Folks had been sent to the penitentiary with football numbers for shit like this. I loved my granny, and I had every intention of hunting down and murdering whoever was responsible for her death, and for killing her in such a foul ass fashion. Still, I had to be realistic in my thought process and deal with the right here and the right now.

I went inside the house in search of a blanket to wrap Granny in. When I walked back outside, the fresh air slapped me out of my stupor and put me in a clearer state of mind. I looked over at Granny's badly beaten face and thought about the horror she must have endured leading up to her death. Her mouth had been wide open when she died; she was in the middle of a scream up under the plastic trash bag. Tears formed in my eyes.

I looked under that lemon tree and thought how cruelly ironic—the one place where I had always been able to find peace and tranquility would now forever be marred by the tragic reality that the woman I loved most in the world had been murdered and buried there. A tear rolled down my cheek. "I'm sorry that I gotta put you back in the ground like this, Granny."

Shug walked up next to me and put his arm around my neck. We stood there side by side in somber silence, each of us lost in our own thoughts. I looked at the dirt-packed mound that had been my chair on so many occasions, and it was as if I could hear the words that my father had written in his letter whispering in my ear.

She told me that you loved to sit up under the lemon tree whenever you were troubled. I'm not surprised. It was also my favorite spot as well. At one time it used to be all flat ground under the lemon tree, but after I made that big move that I mentioned earlier, I left a little something behind.

DEEPLY ROOTED

"Lemme see that letter, Shug." I had been so caught up in my worry for Granny that I had completely put the letter out of my mind.

"What's up?" Shug's antennae were up now.

"In the letter he talks about the ground under the lemon tree." My voice was excited. I unfolded the letter and scanned the paper. "See, right here it says 'The two of you should go dig up under the lemon tree. I left something up under there for the both of you to split down the middle like brothers are supposed to do.'" We both looked at the ground underneath the lemon tree.

"Okay, I'm with you, but where the fuck do we start?" Shug asked.

My eyes scanned the folded paper again. "Look. Right here. See what it says?" I pointed to a line in the letter. *It used to be all flat ground under that lemon tree.* All four of our eyes shifted to the dirt-packed mound, my old chair.

"Hand me that shovel right there," I told Shug and forcefully jammed the sharpened edge into the side of the mound. "Go look in the garage, bruh. It should be another shovel hangin' up on the wall in there," I said over my shoulder as I hurriedly heaved shovel loads of dirt to the side.

Shug joined me a couple of minutes later, and we got after it like it was the thing to do.

Thunk! Thunk!

After a few minutes of digging, the shovel contacted with something that wasn't dirt.

"Right here! Right here, bruh. I got something!" My voice was filled with excitement. My curiosity was an orgy of rich expectations.

"It's a box, I think," Shug guessed when he saw the cardboard.

"Here, pull that side of it," I told him. Together we dislodged the cellophane wrapped box from its earthy grave.

I tore the top off and my heart froze for a second; then it started beating twice as fast as it ever had.

"Look, Wah. It's some more of 'em in there!" Shug hollered out.

Half an hour later, we had all five boxes at our feet and the tops torn off each one. Old school small faces of dead Benjamins stared back at us.

"Pops was a fuckin' beast, bruh!" The statement caught me off guard. Earlier that day Shug made no secret about his profound hatred for our father. I had felt the same way.

Looking at all this money and thinking back to my father's letter where he spoke on how he decided to make a big move in hopes of giving us a better life made me see him in a different light now. He had been eighteen years old with two kids on the way, and he went as big as a street thug could go. There was no doubt in my mind that my father had been a bonafide gangsta in the realest way. There had to be millions in those boxes!

"You're right, bruh. Pops was a fuckin' beast for real!" Then I was saddened by the thought. "It's fucked up though that he never even got a chance to enjoy none of this shit." I shook my head and felt my chest swell with pride at the fact that my father had been on some serious gangsta shit back in the day. Then I felt a rush of sadness come over me at the thought that he had died a poor man's death. Yet, he had millions of dollars sitting right here behind the house he had grown up in.

We stood there talking about it for a minute before reality slapped us back to the here and now. I looked over at Granny's body, and I felt guilty about feeling good. I didn't want to leave here like this but I had to.

"We gotta bury her and get this shit up outta here ASAP, bro!" I told Shug. "Back your truck up into the garage, and let's load this shit up. If the neighbors peep us going back and forth with these boxes, it could raise suspicions and really have us lookin' guilty later on, you feel me?"

"Right, right. That's real talk." He broke out to go get the Escalade.

He backed up into the garage, and I closed the door.

After loading the boxes into the back of the SUV, we buried Granny and took our time cleaning up the backyard, so it didn't look like a crime scene, or a burial ground. Afterward, we did everything we could to cover up the fact that we had ever been there.

I hated having to leave Granny behind like this, but I had to. She had lived a long life, and had a lot of friends. My granny was a good woman, a good person. She deserved a proper funeral, to be laid to rest with dignity and respect. I decided to make an anonymous call so the po-po could find her.

We left up off the block with his Escalade trailing behind my Charger. We were on our way to my crib, a decision mutually agreed on. Shug had people over at his house, whereas I lived alone. The plan was to unload the cargo and divvy up the cheese, 50/50, just like our father had suggested in his letter. It was only right to respect his gangsta. Several times I glanced around as we made our departure. I don't know if Granny's death had me suddenly on edge, but it felt like we were being followed. *Relax*, I commanded the anxiety that flooded my rapidly beating heart.

DEEPLY ROOTED

CHAPTER EIGHTEEN
While the Getting is Good

Wahdatah

Somehow I should have known trouble would follow us once we got our hands on that money. When I banked a left on Euclid, my phone started jumping in my pocket. We had left Granny's with the money two minutes ago.

"What's up wit' it?" It was Shug calling.

"For the last coupla blocks I been noticing a black Toyota Camry a few car lengths back. I think we're being followed, Wah. It's one driver in the car, a dude."

I knew it! "Let's find out fo' sho' if he followin' us. I'ma make a few turns. You keep following me, and we'll know soon enough if that's what it is. If that is the case, then nine times outta ten, it's the same ma'fucka who killed Granny." I grit my teeth and focused on the task at hand.

"I was thinkin' along the same lines, Wah."

"If it is, I'ma air his bitch ass out. On mommas, nigga, he's a dead man!"

"Let's do this," Shug said to me.

"Keep your shit on speaker phone."

"Ai'ight."

I banked a left and drove two blocks. I could see the Camry in my rearview mirror.

"I see his bitch ass, bruh. That ma'fucka definitely is following us." I was talking and checking the rearview at the same time.

"How you wanna do this shit, Wah?"

"I don't wanna draw no unnecessary attention to us while we ridin' wit' all this money, so it gotta be done in an area that ain't got a lot of eyes on us, you feel me?"

"Man, fuck that, homie! He might peep game and push on. Let's get this ma'fucka now while the gettin' is good." It sounded like Shug had a plan of his own.

"Talk to me, bruh. Whatchu' thinkin' on then?" I asked him.

"I say we pull up into a drive-thru, and if he follow us, then you order something and bounce. When I roll up to the window to order something he gon' be a sittin' duck for you, bruh. You get out and come from around the back and clack on his ass."

"That's what's up! I like how you think, Shug. Let's do the damn thang, bruh!" I drove around until I saw a Taco Bell and eased the Charger up to the window and ordered a burrito supreme. I grabbed the bag and pushed the whip away from the drive-thru. Shug drove the Escalade up and took his time with his order. Sure enough, the Camry was right behind him.

As soon as I parked, I jumped out with the fo'-five gripped tightly in my right hand. I ran toward the Camry. The driver inside was so focused on Shug and the Escalade that he never even saw me in the cut. I aimed the chrome canon at the black Camry, and in a full sprint I let the Desert Eagle start bustin' off shots.

Doom! Doom! Doom! Doom! Doom! Doom!

ICE MIKE

Every bullet hit his car and tore the outside of the Camry up. The rear window disintegrated. The back door took four to the body and absorbed the shots. The sixth bullet smashed the front window.

The driver was strapped too.

Boom! Boom! Boom! Boom!

His pistol let off shots in my direction. I could hear bullets whizzing past me and smashing into shit behind me. The Camry's tires burned rubber and crashed into the back of the Escalade trying to get up outta there. My brother was on his shit though. Shug put his truck in reverse and stood up on the gas, preventing the smaller car from escaping. I was about twenty feet away from him. I could see his face clearly now.

Doom! Doom!

The Desert Eagle sounded off with two more thunderous explosions. One of the bullets hit dude in the shoulder. The other one completely destroyed the side view mirror. The Camry went crazy and jumped up on the embankment to his right side.

Boom! Boom!

The driver managed to get off a couple shots as he drove wildly onto the embankment.

Doom!

My next bullet ripped into the back of the headrest and lodged itself somewhere near the nape of his neck, shattering the upper part of his spinal column. He lost control of the Camry and crashed hard into a tree, deploying the airbag. Smoke ascended from under the hood, releasing a loud hissing noise. I slowed down and walked toward the wrecked vehicle in long measured strides. My arm was extended, the fo'-five aimed at the motionless body twisted awkwardly between the front seat and the airbag.

When I walked up on him, his head was turned toward me. Blood poured from his gunshot wounds. He tried to speak but coughed instead, a wet, bloody cough that left him with a red spit bubble formed at his lips. His eyes looked up at me, pleading. He coughed again; more spit and bloody drool ran down his chin. It was obvious he was paralyzed from the neck down. A great amount of evil lived inside his dull black eyes. I knew then that this had to be the person who killed my granny. I didn't want to leave here with any doubts or unanswered questions tormenting my head and heart with 'what ifs'.

"Why you kill my granny? Was it the money?"

He coughed again like he was choking on his own blood and blinked several times. Then he stared up at me and a smile formed on his face. His teeth were stained red with blood, a twinkle of joy shone in his eyes. His sick ass was mocking me!

Doom!

I knocked the twinkle out of his eyes.

Doom! Doom! Click! Click! Click!

My last two shots deflated his head along with the airbag.

"Let's go, bruh. You know somebody done called the po-po by now! Come on! Hurry the fuck up!" Shug hollered and then sped off.

I broke into a sprint and ran as fast as I could toward the Charger. I got the fuck up out of there with the quickness. Shug ended up following me once we linked up a few blocks away from the drive-thru. The back of his Escalade was smashed up good.

After arriving at my spot, he stayed next to the beat up SUV while I carried boxes to my crib one at a time. It was no way on earth we were gonna each carry a box and leave the other boxes unguarded while we were inside.

After all five boxes were resting safely in my living room, only then were we finally able to relax.

"Sit down, Shug. Make yourself at home," I said over my shoulder on my way to the mini-bar. "Whatchu' drinkin' on, bruh?" I asked him.

"A glass of Hennessy wit' some ice in it," he replied and leaned back into the soft leather sofa.

"That's crazy. That's the same shit I be drinkin' on!" I told him as I dropped two ice cubes in each glass. I walked the drinks over and handed him one before taking a seat opposite him.

"To brothers," he proposed a toast.

"To brothers," I responded. Our glasses clinked together, and we tossed back a healthy swig.

"Aahhh!" We both expressed our pleasure at the taste and effect of the liquor. Our laughter was a stress reliever for us both.

After a couple minutes, the room grew quiet with seriousness. My heart broke into a million pieces.

"To Granny, our beloved grandmother, Ms. Mary Mitchell," I said. Our glasses clinked a second time. Another healthy swig down.

Silence fell upon us again, and we both became lost in our own thoughts, defunct in our deliberations. For several moments it was like that, each of us on an emotional journey that took us up and down the highways of hurt and the pathways of pain, through the many streets of sorrows and success, until finally, we ended up coasting down the freeway of a broken family's forlorn and fortune.

The leather sofa sighed under my weight as I sat up close to the edge in preparation for another toast.

"To our father. A man I despised almost all of my life, but who turned out to be a man I should've respected and tried to get to know better," Shug said sadly.

"Everything that you just said. To a bonafide gangsta, our father. A man named Marquis, a thug named Bad Boy." We downed our drinks, and I got up to refill our glasses. I pulled out the embossed solid gold cigar case from one of the openings under the coffee table and held it out to him. He extracted a perfectly rolled blunt. I picked one out too. I put fire to the tip of each one and passed the lighter to him so he could check it out.

"Where you get this ma'fucka from, bruh? I like the fuck outta this." He was referring to the solid gold lighter case with the diamond lining up the sides. The three pea-sized diamonds running up and down each side fit between the fingers perfectly, providing the user with a proper grip when blazing up.

"You like that, bruh?" I asked from behind a thick kush cloud.

"Man, fo' sho', homie. This bitch is the bizness! Is these ma'fuckas real?" He was dumbfounded.

"Ain't that a bitch. I'm offended!" I feigned disgust. "You think that's something?" I asked after deciding to expose my entire hand to him.

After all, he was my brother. We were sitting in a room with five million dollars at our feet. If I couldn't trust him now, I would never be able to trust him.

"Hell yeah! I'd hit a nigga upside the head with the pistol for a joint like this here!" he proclaimed loudly and laughed. I believed him too. His reputation wasn't nothing nice.

"That ain't shit, Shug," I told him and stood up. Another cloud of kush smoke enveloped me, and then briefly trailed behind me before vanishing into the air after I walked away. I disappeared for a few seconds before I came back to the living room with the briefcase in tow. I sat back down and set the briefcase on the tabletop. Again I hit the blunt and spoke through the smoke around my head after I clicked the briefcase open.

"Tell me what you think about this then." I flipped it open and slowly turned it.

Shug's eyes got as big as golf balls. His mouth opened wide with amazement.

"Yeah, that's what she said." I laughed and took another pull on the blunt. I chased the kush smoke with a swig of Henny and leaned back into the softness of the sofa, loving how I was feeling at the moment.

"Damn, Wahdatah. I shoulda been fuckin' witchu' instead of feudin' witchu', man. I ain't know you was gettin' it like this!"

"I wasn't, bruh. I just hit a lick with the homies Moolah and Thun-Thun." I got quiet when I thought about how my homeboys had gotten smacked up.

"What's wrong, Wah?"

"Moolah and Thun-Thun got smoked after we hit the lick while we was gettin' away."

"Aw damn, that's fucked up. Sorry to hear that, bro." He was sincere when he said it. I could see it in his eyes.

"I know, man. Them niggas was solid soldiers, bruh. It's just hella sad that they ain't even here to enjoy this shit. You feel me? We supposed to all be up in here countin' these big faces and plottin' on what we gon' splurge on with this shit."

"That's real. I feel you on that. What kinda plans you got with all this bling, bruh?"

"I was plannin' on slangin' it to my Sicilian connect, but now that's on hold."

"What happened?"

"I gotta wait for my boy Drape to get off this house arrest shit before I can move it."

"Why's that?" Shug hit his blunt hard and held it in.

"Because, when Moolah and Thun-Thun got bapped I ain't have no security. My boy Drape can't leave the house without the po-po knowing everywhere he been, because it's a GPS in that monitor, and I don't trust my connect enough to do the deal without no security. Not with all this cheese on the line."

"I feel you, bruh. That makes sense. How long before your boy Drape get up off that house arrest shit?"

"A little over two weeks."

"Bruh, you ain't gotta wait that long. I got you! Shit, if you want to, me and my nigga Camron can provide you with security. That's what the fuck we do, Wah!" Shug sat up and rubbed his hands together.

ICE MIKE

My mind flashed back to when we were at the IHOP, and he signaled somebody outside.

"Talk to me about exactly what it is that y'all do," I said, fully interested in his proposal. I wasn't trying to be sitting around holding onto a briefcase full of jewelry when it was hot as fuck out there in the streets. If I could get this shit off now, then the sooner the better. But don't nothing come free in my world.

"How much is it gonna cost me, bruh?" I asked him.

He put the blunt to his lips and puffed on it, holding the potent smoke in his chest for as long as his lungs would allow. Shug blew it out slowly and looked me in the eyes before he spoke.

"I'm offended that you would suggest such a thing." He feigned disgust the same way I did a few minutes ago.

We laughed hard and slapped each other's hands.

"Touché, my nigga. Touché." I gave him that.

"That's what brothers do, right?"

"What's that?" I asked.

"Have each other's back, regardless," he said.

"That's what's up! Ay." I paused with a question.

"What it do?"

"Let's count this shit up and see what the total look like." I nodded toward the boxes.

"Man, you ain't said nothin' but a word, nerd!"

"Nerd? That's what I ain't." I raised up and left the living room again. I came back with a money-counting machine.

"I figure since it's five boxes, and they all weigh about the same, then all we gotta do is count one box and multiply it by five, then we split it in half. Either that, or we both take two boxes and just split the fifth box down the middle." I set the machine down on the table next to the briefcase and the pistol.

"Like I said, bruh. Nerd!"

"Fuck you."

The trees and Hennessy helped lighten the mood and relax us. It seemed to loosen up our tongues as well.

"I ain't gon' lie, Wah. I'ma keep it one hundred witchu'. Growing up, I hated the shit out of you. Real talk, I seriously despised you, homie. But no matter how much I disliked you, bruh, your suit-wearin' ass always went against the grain. I admire that . . . shows character."

I half-grinned as I sat there and let him talk. I wanted to hear how he really felt about me when we were enemies.

"When everybody else in the streets was sportin' creased up khaki suits and Chuck Taylor's; you were stylishly rockin' silk Armani suits and expensive dress shoes. It didn't matter what the occasion was either. Whenever I saw you out and about you was always makin' a fashion statement. I guess I always admired the fact that you were different like that, Wah." He downed the rest of his drink and refilled his glass to the halfway point.

"I never would've guessed that you felt that way, bruh. I appreciate your honesty, Shug. Shit, since we keepin' it all the way one hundred with each other, I'ma keep it clean witchu' too." I hit my blunt hella hard and stifled a cough before continuing. "I hated you the same way, man. But despite how I felt about you back in the day your swag told niggas to back the fuck up and take notice. The confidence you carry is something I've always respected about you. Your swag is official, playboy, and that's real talk, bruh."

Those heartfelt admissions seemed to open up the floodgates. We ended up staying up late into the night until the sun rudely interrupted us. After counting the money and determining that it was roughly five million dollars, we spent the rest of the night chopping it up, getting to know each other on some real shit. He told me some more of his life story. I told him some more of mine.

Our stories paralleled each other's in an uncanny sense. It went far beyond us sharing the same father.

Before he bounced, we made plans to hook up later that day, so we could do the handshake and hug thing with each other's people. We also had to sit down and formulate a game plan on how best to go about doing a deal with my connect, Joey Cheese. I wanted to get these jewels up off me as soon as possible.

When I lay back on the silk sheets and sank my head into the soft goose down pillows, I thought about how crazy it was that I got to know my brother more in the last twenty-four hours than I had in the last twenty-three years. Then I thought about my Granny and cried like I hadn't cried since I was a little kid. Finally, sleep overtook me and rescued me from my misery—those repetitive thoughts of impending death and how much time was left in my own life.

DEEPLY ROOTED

CHAPTER NINETEEN
Now That's What I Call Gangsta

Wahdatah

My cell phone was blowing up in my ear. It was some time in the middle of the day, and sleep was being hella good to me. I hated having to stir from my slumber, but I grabbed the Rolex and shook my head to clear my vision. The drink and the kush had a way of putting a nigga into a sleep-induced coma sometimes.

It was 4:03 PM.

Damn, I had slept all day. It was probably going to take me a day or two to get my body back on track with my normal routine.

I picked the phone up without looking at it as soon as it started ringing again.

"Hello, who this?" I answered impatiently, still mad that the constant ringing had awakened me.

"Oh, it's like that now?" It was Tocarra. I had been ignoring her calls. "You still trippin'?" she asked.

I recognized her voice immediately. Sweet and syrupy, soft like a Sade song.

"Naw, it ain't like that, Tocarra. I ain't trippin' off that shit." My dick was rock hard as freaky visions of her flawless body ran around naked in my head. "I stayed up late last night, and it caught up to me. I'm actually just now wakin' up."

"Well, I just wanted to call and make peace with you, Wahdatah. I don't want to fight with you, and if that's the reason you've been avoiding me, then I want to apologize and squash the beef. I don't mean any disrespect when I ask you all those questions. I'm just trying to get to know you, the real you, because I'm just trying to get to know exactly what I'm getting myself into before I start catching feelings. So I apologize for coming off as being the nosy type chick."

After she finished I played it cool and stayed silent.

"That's hella messed up, Wah. I apologize to you, and you sit there and don't say shit. You are so wrong for that!" Anger and hurt dripped from her every word.

"Naw, naw, it ain't even like that, Tocarra."

"Then what is it? Why aren't you saying anything?"

"I'll tell you later, after I come scoop you up, if that's okay with you? I want to take you to a function. Show off the woman I want to be with. That is, if you want to be with me. I accept your apology as well. It was petty and we're bigger than that. So what's up? Are we gon' kick it?" My words were spoken in a way that caressed her anger. She could hear the smile in my words and feel the hug in my voice. I clearly understood the persuasive power of a good dick-down. I knew she was like putty in my hands right now." I meant every word I said too. Tocarra had her feminine swag turnt all the way up.

"What makes you think I want to be your girl like that, Wahdatah?" she joked.

"Because, I got you open, and you're feelin' me as much as I'm feelin' you." She wasn't prepared for my uncut honesty.

"Boy, you crazy." Her weak comeback let me know that I had won this round.

"Real talk, Tocarra. I want to make you my girl and be that dude in your life that completes you. I also want to introduce you to some of my peoples."

"Like that?" she said, surprised.

"Yup, like that. But the invitation only stands if you choose."

"Hmmm, let me think about it, Wah." She giggled girlishly. "Okay. Yes, I'll be your girl."

"That's what's up, ma. Wear something casual and be ready around sixish, okay?"

"Okay then, I'll be ready."

"Stay sexy, baby girl, and keep a nigga in your thoughts when you get dressed."

"That won't be hard to do. I think it's safe to say that you've been in them a lot lately. Kinda took over and got comfortable in 'em too."

"I like that. I ain't gon' front; the feeling is mutual. I'll pick you up at six, ai'ight?"

"I'll be ready."

"Ai'ight, ma."

"Bye, Wahdatah."

I ended the call and went straight to the shower.

After getting fresh and clean, I put together a lil' something to eat: eggs, turkey bacon, hash browns, toast and orange juice. Breakfast for dinner!

DEEPLY ROOTED

I'ma thug through and through, but getting paper and having style ain't never been a problem with me. My sense of fashion always been stylish with a swaggish flair. I stepped into a pair of black Marc Jacobs slacks, tucked the wife beater in, and chose an off-white button down shirt. The matching Timbs and Yankees fitted cap had me on point. I called it my 'Book Look'. I slipped the Rolex on and hung a nice thick platinum rope around my neck. I let it hang to showcase the hand-sized diamond encrusted cross.

After reloading the fo'-five, I put an extra clip in my pocket and snatched up my cell phone and keys. A lot of things lay on my plate. I had a gang of shit to handle before I scooped up Tocarra and met up with Shug and his people. *I miss my granny already! Where the fuck am I gonna hide $2.5 million? I gotta catch up with Joey Cheese. My boy Drape waiting on me to come holler at him.*

For the next two hours, I organized and compartmentalized my agenda. Put money aside for Granny's funeral. Stuffed the rest of the money in a suitcase and pushed it to the back of my closet. Hid the briefcase behind the refrigerator. Called Drape and ran everything down to him about how shit had popped off over the course of the last two days.

When I locked the door and walked toward the Mopar Charger, I held a fly ass diamond earring set with a matching tennis bracelet and watch in my hand. *Tocarra gon' love this!* It was gorgeous, a gang of flawless diamonds surrounded by a bunch of platinum. The jewelry store heist made it easy for me to bear these types of gifts.

At ten minutes to six, I parked in front of Tocarra's crib. I leaned on the horn twice. I opened the door and Trey

Songz gave the block a free concert, courtesy of the four fifteens in the trunk.

Tocarra stepped out of her house wearing a body hugging watermelon red Tube dress that stopped mid-thigh. Ass on swoll. Titties pushed up and poking out, demanding my eyes pay attention to them. Her face was meticulously made-up. Hair, stylishly bunched atop her head. A long wisp of hair hung down the front, hiding one of her pretty eyes. Thankfully, she wasn't wearing anything extravagant in the way of accessories.

I walked up to her, and we hugged. I could tell she missed me. She could tell I missed her too. When I hugged her and squeezed her ass, the kiss we shared afterward was sensuous and passionate. Loud with moans and soft grunts of pleasure.

After kissing for a minute, we put a little space between us so we could breathe.

"Take this off, ma." I gently removed her earrings, necklace, and watch. "Let me put this on you." I hit her ears, neck, and wrist off with something exquisite and expensive.

She was putty in my hands, slowly being molded into my kind of chick, a piece of the puzzle that was necessary for my happiness. Tocarra looked deep into my eyes.

"Thank you so much, baby! They are so beautiful. I love it! You know you didn't have to do this, right?" Her response pleased me. My dimples were on full display. She bent low and looked at her reflection in the side view mirror.

"C'mon now. I know I didn't have to do it, Tocarra. I wanted to do it."

She pushed me up against the passenger side door and we kissed again for a minute

"Damn, that tasted good. Gimme another one." I kissed her harder, with more urgency. Trey Songz voice serenaded the occasion.

"Oh shit, Wah! You makin' me hot!" She pushed herself away and fluffed her hair. "Let's go, before we do something that ends up on YouTube."

I opened the door for her, and within minutes I was whipping the Charger in and out of traffic. She sang along to every Trey Songz track that banged out the system. Her voice was beautiful too. *What can't this girl do?*

"Why me, Tocarra?" I asked the question out of the blue, talking over the music.

"Why you what?" She turned and looked at me. A smile formed on her lips. She placed her hand on my thigh and turned the volume down a bit, waiting for my response.

"Why does a good girl like you want to be around a bad boy like me?" I asked and adjusted the rearview mirror before turning the music all the way down. I looked into her eyes and got lost in them for a few seconds, mesmerized.

"Because you're light-skinned with light-brown eyes."

"C'mon, ma. I'm for real. Dead ass."

Tocarra sighed lightly. "Okay. This is real talk. Wah, you're confident and self-assured. You're attractive and considerate. You're strong and handsome. You're tough, but at the same time you are so gentle with me when you need to be. You're a good listener and a great talker. But more than any other reason, I was initially attracted to you because you made the best first impression on me that any man ever has, and that won me over from the get-go." She leaned closer and kissed me on the cheek, and then affectionately caressed my jaw.

"First impression?" I asked, surprised at that revelation. "What first impression is this that you're referring to?"

She laughed softly, almost like a girlish giggle. "The day we met, in front of my house at the cab. You took your time and practically seduced me, and on top of all that you were a gentleman. And you held the door open for me. You did all of that after robbing a jewelry store, being shot at, and eluding the police." She squeezed my thigh and leaned close again. "Now that's what I call gangsta!" she whispered in my ear. Her lips grabbed hold of my earlobe, and her probing tongue almost made me lose control of the Charger.

I was dumb struck by her response. How the hell did she know?

"How the hell you figure I robbed a jewelry store and was running from the police?" I asked, still not fully recovered from the shock of her answer.

"I'm a writer, Wahdatah. I have a very active imagination, boo. When I saw the story on the news that night and I replayed our first encounter, I put two and two together. Your eyes gave you up, too. You kept looking to see where that helicopter was while you ran your game on me. I played with myself all night when I replayed that shit back in my head." Her laugh made me laugh.

"Wow, so that's why you asked all those questions. You wanted to see how honest I'd be." I turned the Charger down Shug's block.

"Yup, I'm guilty as charged. Besides, I'm not always a good girl. I can be bad too when I have to be."

DEEPLY ROOTED

The way she said it sucked me in further. I was really falling for her.

* * * * *

When I knocked on the heavy wooden door, I could hear Rick Ross rapping about Maybach Music. A beautiful, light-skinned chick opened the door. I remembered her from the theater the other day. She had been hanging off Shug's arm looking like a video vixen.

Damn! I thought, while my expression remained unreadable. Shug's face popped up over her shoulder.

"Come on in, Wah. Make yourself at home, bruh." We hugged and dapped each other. "Turn that shit down for a minute!" he yelled to somebody.

Tocarra stood next to me wearing a shocked expression.

When everybody else in the room saw us standing there, they too had shocked looks. I couldn't conceal my smile.

In all, there were six of us. The same six who had stood in a tense standoff just a few days ago in the concession line at the movie theater. It was obvious he hadn't told his people anything about us.

"Chill, chill, chill y'all," he spoke over the buzz of confused whispering that broke out. "Check this out, man." He put his arm around my neck and pulled me off to the side, a couple feet away from the crowd.

"Ay y'all. I know this is obviously a shock to all of you, just as it was a shock to me yesterday. So let me bring you up to speed on what's really good." He took his arm from around my neck. "For twenty-three years I walked around this world thinking I was an only child. For over half that time I was beefin' with this cat right here. It ain't no secret, as you all know, we were sworn enemies and hated each other's guts. Yesterday though, I found out that we were brothers, blood brothers—same blood. Me and Wah have the same father."

Everybody in the room sucked in some air and looked around the room with confusion. The beautiful, light-skinned chick who had answered the door stared at me with a fascinating look in her eyes.

He turned to the dime piece who had opened the door. "This is my brother, Wahdatah. Wah, this is my other half, Miko, my thug missus." The light-skinned chick was smiling now, only this time she had a twinkle in her eyes. The smile threw me off a little.

"Hi." Her introduction was simple. Her overall look was hot, but there was something about her that screamed *boss bitch!*

"What's up? Pleasure to meet you." We shook hands. She caught me off guard when she pulled me close and pressed her soft body up against me, hugging me hard.

"We family now, so the pleasure is all mine, *Wah*." She said my name like she was being facetious.

Next, I met Camron and his girl Monisha. Then I introduced all of them to Tocarra. Tocarra's face lit up when I introduced her as my girlfriend. Afterward, I pulled Tocarra to the side and broke everything down to her. I explained it all, from the letter to the lemon tree. I left out all the grimy shit though.

We fired up blunts and blew some bomb kush that smelled like blueberries. Tocarra and I shared a blueberry blunt and spoke in depth about our mutual desire to establish a stronger bond.

All six of us smoked, drank, and conversed late into the night until we knocked out sometime in the wee hours of the morning.

The next day after making that anonymous phone call from a payphone, I got a phone call from the authorities informing me that my grandmother had been found dead in her backyard under the lemon tree, murdered by an unknown assailant. I acted distraught, which wasn't hard to do.

Later that day I hollered at my brother and told him what he already knew. Together we made plans for her funeral service and burial. Out of respect for Granny, we put everything that we currently had our hands in on the back burner for the time being. We wanted to respect her memory and send Granny off right.

After the funeral, we planned on putting our boot prints all over the Southeast Planet streets. Everybody in the city was going to know that Wah and Shug wasn't nothing to be fucked with.

We were young. We were rich. And we were hungry street savages ready to leave our boot prints on the game.

CHAPTER TWENTY
Shit Out of Luck

One week later . . .

Although it had only been a week since Granny had been laid to rest, a part of me felt like it had been buried with her. The only thing that I had left in this world now was my brother. It's crazy that I felt that way because I was sittin' on $2.5 million and holding on to a briefcase full of diamonds and jewelry. But with Granny gone now, my heart had a hole in it. It just goes to show you that family is priceless.

We sat around the table in my crib four deep, huddled up under a thick cloud of kush smoke, plotting on thug business.

"Shug, you say this is the type of shit you and Camron do on a regular basis, so let's put yo' skills to the test, bruh. I think the wisest move would be to set a meeting up with Joey Cheese first. You feel me? Get a temperature check and see how he talkin'. If he don't want to bend on his price and holla with the right numbers, I'ma just say fuck it and go somewhere else with this shit. Right now, the way I see it is: I'm dealin' with this cat from a position of strength, so I can afford to push a hard line and max out what I'm willing to settle for." I made eye contact with Shug and winked. "Me and Drape discussed it, and that's how we feel about it."

DEEPLY ROOTED

"Okay, that's all good, bruh, and I can work around that. What we gon' do is roll witchu' to the sit-down. Me and you gon' go up in there and pow-wow wit' 'em face to face to see what he talkin' about. Camron is gon' be in the cut out of sight, but well within shootin' range, ya' dig? Also, I'ma slap these on him." He set two flat pea-sized objects in front of us on top of the table.

"What the fuck are those?" Drape asked.

"Recording devices. Miniature recording devices that can be conveniently attached to articles of clothing. For instance, when I walk up on you and shake your hand, then hug you and pound your back like this, you don't even know that you been tagged." He gave a demonstration and inconspicuously attached the device onto Drape's clothing. It looked like a piece of lint or something.

"What if he ain't wearing black though?" I quizzed him, noticing that all the devices were black.

"Then Camron is gonna notify me beforehand through my earpiece of what color I need to use." He pulled out pairs in damn near every color.

"That's what's up then. Shit, I like how that sound."

"If it get ugly up in there, Wah, you gotta trust my nigga Cam, bruh. He don't play. He's a dead shot, and he don't miss. When one of them mafia ma'fuckas fall over, that's when you go for your shit and bust off until everybody in the room is dead. We normally use a code word when we do our dirty, and that's the green light for Camron to start pickin' people off."

"Code word? Ai'ight, like what?" I asked, feeling the smoothness in the way he laid out his plan.

"Shit out of luck. When you say the words 'shit out of luck' expect er' one of them Mafioso's heads to explode. Don't hesitate, bruh, or it could be the last mistake you ever make."

"Shit out of luck, huh?"

"It's lights out after that."

"That's what's up. I'ma call his ass now, set up a meeting, and see what it do." I pulled out the cell phone.

"Make it happen, bruh. We ready."

Ring. Ring. Ring.

The Mafioso's phone was ringing.

"Yeah?" The thick Sicilian accent was definitely Joey Cheese's.

"What's good, Joey Cheese? This ya boy, Wahdatah."

"Wahdatah, Wahdatah. Fuck yous been hiding out at?"

"Ain't no hidin' out over here, Joey. Just stayin' out the way until the heat dies down, you feel me? Two of my boys died doing this thang, Joey. That's two murders that I ain't trying to have pinned on me. You know how the games go."

"Yeah, I do. So let's cut to the fuckin' chase, Wahdatah. You know what I'm sayin'?" It was all business with him. He didn't give a fuck about my homies getting murked in the process.

"I want two million for this shit, Joey. Two million or I'll take my business elsewhere." I figured if I started off at two million and got it, I'd win big. But if I ended up having to settle for $1.5 million I was still winning, because a week ago I would've settled for a cool million for the diamonds and other jewelry.

"That's a lot of money, kid. No way can I come off a that much cash without seeing the merchandise first."

"Choose a place and time," I said. He gave me a time and location.

* * * * *

The best expectations to have is none. When making any deal concerning a lot of dough, even the most standup guy will turn on you. I kept that in mind later that day when we pushed into the cheap motel parking lot and went to meet up with the mobster.

"Joey Cheese! It's good to see you again, my man. This is my brother Shug. I'm sure you understand my desire to have him with me." I shook his hand and hugged him.

They shook hands and hugged. Shug was good at what he did. He slapped the recording devices on with ease.

Joey offered us drinks and a cigar. I passed on the cigar and chose to sip on some Hennessy.

After a few minutes of small talk, we got down to the meat of the matter. I popped open the briefcase and pushed it over to him. His bushy eyebrows arched with surprise.

"Nice . . . I like it already, but it's definitely not worth two million of my dollars." The mobster stated dryly after he played with a few pieces of jewelry before setting the pieces back into the briefcase.

I stood and reached into my suit pocket, pulled out the black velvet bags, and dumped the diamonds onto the table.

Joey motioned to one of his henchmen, and a weasel-faced, skinny dude wearing a pair of bifocals stepped up close. He took an appraisal instrument out of his pocket and attached it to his eye socket after removing the bifocals.

One by one he picked up the stones, rolled them around between his thumb and index finger and eyeballed them meticulously. He was estimating its value, checking its clarity. Appraising my stash.

After he finished, he leaned over and whispered into Joey Cheese's right ear for a few seconds.

"Still not worth two million of my dollars, Wahdatah."

I laughed and snorted. "I figured you'd say some shit like that." Then I poured the other bag of diamonds out.

"You sly dog you!" Joey pointed a fat finger at me and laughed. Then he motioned to his guy again.

Same process, stone by stone. Same results.

"The best that I can offer you is one million flat." His voice was dry and empty, like he wasn't all that impressed or interested. His eyes kept peeking at the pile of diamonds though.

"One point seven-five, Joey. This is over three million dollars' worth of jewelry here. Man!" I insisted.

We haggled for a few minutes until we both agreed to settle on $1.5 million. We made plans to meet again soon.

As soon as we walked out of the motel room, it all went bad. Their conversation was being monitored by Camron. When we got into the car, he played back the conversation that had taken place in the motel right after we bounced.

Joey Cheese: *I want you to rent this same room for one more day, Santino. I don't want anybody else in here except you and Franky, capish? I'm gonna set up a second meeting with that tough talkin', smug, rug head, and we're gonna take those damn stones from him. Kill him and that fuckin' monkey ass brother of his.*

DEEPLY ROOTED

Santino: *Okay boss, consider it done. How do you want us to dispose of the bodies, Joey?*

Joey Cheese: *Get the fuck outta here, Santino. Mob style, you friggin' idiot. Pop! One time to the back of the fuckin' head and leave 'em stinkin' in a friggin' river. Badabing Badaboom.*

Santino: *Sure thing, boss, sure thing.*

* * * * *

The call meant for my death and the theft of my jewels came just after 1 PM the next day. Joey Cheese wanted to meet, same place same time.

"No problem, Joey, but plan on staying a while because I'ma bring my money-counting machine. No disrespect, but my associates want to be extra careful about this. They want me to count all of the money first before we hand over the jewelry." I hit him with that to ensure that he actually brought the money with him. If he had plans on killing us, then it was also plausible that he might not feel the need to bring any of the money.

"Of course, Wahdatah. I understand. It's the nature of the business."

Later that day, we were in the same motel room facing each other with smiles of the most deceptive kind. I had the money-counting machine on the small table in front of me. On the bed was a gym bag full of big faces.

"Hand me a stack so I can make sure this raggedy ma'fucka still works, Joey," I told him. I wanted to make sure there was actually real money in the gym bag. As far as Joey knew, the plan was for me to call Shug once I counted the money. Only then would he enter the room with the

169

briefcase full of bling. But right now I was the only one in the motel room with the three mobsters.

He reached over and unzipped the bag. Then he threw a stack of big faces on the table and continued to puff on his cigar. I picked up the stack and fed it into the machine.

"It looks like you're shit out of luck, Joey," I said to the Mafioso. He looked at me like I was stupid.

"What the fuck are you—"

Thoooomp!

A fine mist of blood spray hit me on the side of my face as soon as Joey Cheese's head burst open. His body fell forward and landed with a loud thud at my feet. My chrome was in my hand before a puddle of blood could start forming under his body.

Doom! Doom!

The Desert Eagle roared, and two bullets smacked Franky in the chest. His body slammed into the wall and slid slowly to the floor. He sat on his back pockets, mouth and eyes wide in death.

Santino looked at me like he couldn't believe it was actually going down like this. His eyes ping-ponged between his two dead mob cronies.

Doom!

My canon crushed the front row of his pearly whites. The back of his neck splashed against the wall behind him. His body went limp and fell to the floor, hard.

Thump!

I threw the money-counting machine into the gym bag and stood up to leave when I heard somebody beating on the motel room door.

DEEPLY ROOTED

Who the fuck is that? was the thought that crossed my mind. I was about to open it up, thinking it was Shug or Camron. My hand touched the doorknob.

"Joey, is everything all right in there, boss?" The thick Sicilian accent was unmistakable. Joey Cheese must have had one of his soldiers outside in the cut just in case shit got ugly.

Doom! Doom! Doom! Doom!

I held the chrome sideways, busting plugs out the door. I heard a soft moan on the other side of the thin wooden door. The fo'-five getting off in the small space had my ears ringing.

Doom! Doom!

Two more shots through the door just to make sure. I tried to peek through the six holes in the door, but I couldn't see shit. *Fuck it!* I grabbed the doorknob and flung the door open with the fo'-five pointed straight ahead. A young Italian guy was laid out on his back with bloody holes in the front of his white sweats. I hurried and switched out the used clip with a fresh one. I heard the sound of shoes pounding on the pavement.

Oh shit! It's some more! I thought and raised the cannon up to squeeze some off.

"Chill! Chill! Chill, Wah, it's me!" My brother had his Glock 9 up and aimed, ready to dump.

"Let's get the fuck outta here!" I yelled to him.

He busted a U-turn in mid-stride, and broke fast toward the car. I was right behind him with the gym bag clutched tightly in my hand. I tossed the bag through the open back window and jumped into the car. Shug was already in the passenger seat.

"Who the fuck was that clown?" Shug asked, his eyes wild with confusion. He hadn't planned on that extra soldier being there, and it pissed him off. "Fuck! Fuck! Fuck! I shoulda thought of that, man!" He two-pieced the dash with his fist as Camron sped off.

I looked out the back window and saw a group of nosy spectators emerging from their rooms. "Let it go, bruh. It's a lesson learned. You feel me?" I tried to calm him down.

"Fuck that shit, Wah. Mistakes like that get niggas murked, man!"

"I feel you on that, bruh. But it is what it is. What's done is done. It's a lesson learned, homie." I put my hand on his shoulder and shook him. "Shake that shit off, bruh. Real talk, it's a lesson learned."

"You coulda got smoked though, Wah!" he muttered, and rested his elbow against the door with his chin between his index finger and thumb. It was hella obvious the shit was eating him up.

We rode in silence for a block or two before I decided to squash the uneasy vibe. "Look here, Shug. Here go 1.5 million reasons that say tonight was a good night." I unzipped the gym bag and poured the contents all over his head and shoulders. Stacks of big faces fell onto his lap and down to the floor of the car. "What's done is done. We all good, family!" I hollered and tried to laugh it off.

Camron joined in too. It took a few seconds, but Shug eventually laughed along with us as well.

All things considered, it went pretty good; this thing with Joey Cheese. We got away with the money and still had the jewelry. Hopefully we didn't leave behind any evidence that would put the po-po on our trail, or even worse, somehow put the mob and Joey Cheese's people on us.

Damn, did that fat mafucka tell his people that he was dealing with us? Did the Costra Nostra know that Joey Cheese was doing business with me? Shug was trippin' on the dead Mafioso soldier, but I was trippin' on the living mob soldiers who might come hunting for me.

CHAPTER TWENTY-ONE
Empire State

Wahdatah

Three weeks later . . .

The homie Drape was finally off house arrest, and to celebrate his newfound freedom, we decided to go see what the Empire State had to offer some California thugs.

We stepped off the private jet I rented like famous folk. Eight deep, swag turnt all the way up, and an air of gangsta mixed with something sexy floating around us as we made our way down the steps. The Big Apple embraced us in true New York fashion; snowflakes falling, carried on a soft wind. The cold November wind chill biting into our sun-kissed California skin.

"This is what the fuck I'm talkin' about!" Drape had a beautiful, thick, light-skinned chick on his arm. He had finally cut that hood rat Carmelita loose, and knocked a sistah that appeared to have a lil something going for herself. Petra was her name. Think Lisa Raye with a fatter ass and bigger tits.

"Yes sir! I been wantin' to take a bite out of the Big Apple for a good minute now. On the rizeal, my nigga, I'm tryin' to see what all the ma'fuckin' hoopla is about." Camron had his arm wrapped around the small of

Monisha's back, ensuring she maintained her balance on the slick, icy surface of the tarmac.

Shug and Miko walked like royalty through the airport.

Tocarra and I walked close together, her arm around my waist, and mine draped casually across her slender shoulders.

We had come to New York to do a little shopping, at least that was the impression the girls were under. Us hard-headed hood fellas were still trying to move this briefcase full of jewelry. Shug knew somebody who knew somebody.

When we walked through the airport, a clean-cut, brown-skinned brotha held up a sign inquiring about the Mitchell party arriving at JFK. He led us to our awaiting vehicles. The pair of pearl white limousines waited patiently at the curb for us. Me, Shug, Tocarra, and Miko ducked our heads and got comfortable in the back of the first stretch limo. Drape, Camron, Monisha, and Petra filled the second one. The luxury whips jumped off the curb and merged into traffic like a knife cutting butter.

As soon as we got into the flow of traffic, I held a flute full of champagne up and proposed a toast. "To the good life, y'all."

"To the good life!" everybody exclaimed loudly in unison.

The mood was festive. Laughter came hella easy. Kendrick Lamar's "Money Tree" was beating through the speakers, saying something about 'money ain't a thang'.

After getting settled in our rooms at the Hilton, we hit up every high-end store up and down Fifth Avenue with a dogged determination to fuck off every big face in our possession. The stacks were burning holes in our pockets.

ICE MIKE

Like a school of stylishly dressed fish, we swam in a well-synchronized group to the most coveted shops: Louis Vuitton, Gucci, Chanel, Prada, Dior. You name it. If it sold expensive designer clothing, the women found it.

For the better part of a day, we shut the stores down. Walking back to the limo with four bags in each hand, it became abundantly clear to me that for the women, shopping was like a sport. Their competitive juices kicked in, and they took on entirely different personalities.

When inside the stores, it didn't matter whether they were on carpet, or highly polished marble floors; they maintained their speed and executed their route-running like elite professional athletes. On the drive back to the hotel, the chatter was incessant with victorious celebration. They popped bottles and boasted to one another about their individual shining moments on the field of play. Their celebratory demeanor was reminiscent of when we bodied Joey Cheese and his crew and got away with the 1.5 mil'.

Thankfully, none of them put up much of a fuss when we all declined to hit the clubs with them later that night. They had their plans and we had ours.

* * * * *

"What the fuck is takin' your boy so long, Shug?" The ground around us was blanketed with snow and the wind was blowing hard at a sideways angle. "We been out here waitin' for twenty minutes, bruh." The cold weather was pissing me off, evident by the mean-mug I sported.

"He'll be here in a minute, bruh. Relax. He just texted me and told me that traffic was crazy."

I blew my warm breath into my closed fist and tried to defrost my fingers. My other hand had the briefcase in a choke hold. "I think that's him right there." Shug nodded in the direction of a slow approaching dude in a hoodie. My eyes followed his finger, and right off the top I went to measuring the New York dude named Hasan up. First impressions could be a life or death assessment.

"What's good, son?" His New York accent was hella thick, and his appearance was typical New York thug— hoodie over a fitted hat, baggy jeans, and Timbs. I was still waiting on that first impression vibe to complete the assessment process and send back its results.

We did the introduction dance, handshakes and hugs, and then fell in line when he told us to follow him.

"Did you get those thumpers that I mailed to you?" Shug asked him.

"No doubt, duke. Here." Hasan passed the pistols to Shug who passed them to the respective owner. Everybody checked their strap to make sure it was loaded.

Homeland security was on their job, so mailing the guns to Hasan ahead of our arrival took care of the customs situation.

A few minutes later, we were at the bottom of a four-step stairwell. Hasan was beating the side of his fist against a heavy metal door.

Seconds later, a slot slid open and two blood shot beady eyes appeared.

"What's ya bizness?" Gruff. All business, no bullshit.

"It's Hasan. I came to holla at Keitho. We got an appointment." Hasan's first impression results were just in; somewhat suspect and not to be trusted. It was a gut feeling.

ICE MIKE

Someone unlocked the heavy metal door from the other side. As cold as it was outside, I just knew that it would be warm inside once the door clanged shut. How wrong I was. It was a fucking icebox in there!

When the doorman went to search us it got hostile.

"Hold up, potna, we ain't comin' off our thumpers, bruh? It's too much at stake here, folks. Too much money on the line." I stiffed-armed dude and handled my fo'-five.

Dude told us to wait and left the room. Then he returned and posted back up. He ice grilled me. I smirked and laughed at him before turning my back to let him know it wasn't no fear on mine.

"This way, y'all," another hard-faced thug with a gun appeared out of nowhere and instructed us with a deep voice.

Instinctively, my free hand hugged on the fo'-five. I saw everybody in my crew doing the same thing. We followed the deep voiced thug around a corner, down a long corridor, and around another corner. He stopped in front of an office door, knocked twice, and twisted the doorknob.

When we entered the office, I was thankful to feel the heat hit my body. My hand stayed clutching the chrome though.

Keitho was a big burly Biggie Smalls lookin' cat with short dreads that looked like black French fries on his head. The scar that ran from his earlobe to the corner of his mouth was shiny proof that somebody had tried their damnedest to cut his ass.

My nostrils were assaulted with the strong smell of chronic smoke and something else that I couldn't quite put my finger on yet. It was a sweet, funky, pungent odor that forced me to start breathing through my mouth.

"Walk wit' me, fam'," Keitho said to us. He turned and walked through a beaded curtain. Lights flickered, and that smell overwhelmed both of my nostrils, and then it flipped my stomach upside down. I fought off the urge to gag when my eyes finally adjusted to the scene before me.

A big ass German shepherd was fucking the shit out of some unlucky dark-skinned dude whose wrists were shackled to a chain coming out of the wall. His ankles were handcuffed to metal rings bolted down to the floor.

The German shepherd had mounted him from the back, and was literally fucking the shit out of him doggie-style. Fast, furious, hard strokes. Tongue wagging and slobbering all over the unlucky dude's back.

The chronic smoke came from the blunt that Keitho was puffing on. The strong, sweet smell emitted from the scented candles that burned slowly. The funky odor was caused from the shit spilling out of dude's ass as the dog humped him without mercy.

"Aw, man, what the fuck is up with that shit!" Hasan asked. I was glad that none of my crew had asked the question. That woulda made us seem a little squeamish, a way I wasn't trying to look or seem at this juncture of the game, in a city across the country, in a building underground doing business with heartless New York goons.

Right then I decided I wasn't feeling Hasan none. Keitho stopped and turned to face us.

"That bitch ass sucka right there thought it was okay to dog my baby sister out and fuck around on her, so he gettin' exactly what he gave her. Fucked by a dog ass nigga. Karma's a bitch? Ain't that right, dog ass nigga?" Keitho's laugh was sick and sinister.

The man on the floor cried out in pain. The dog barked loud and humped harder.

We followed Keitho into an office and took a seat after him. "These are—" Hasan started to say.

"I can speak for myself, bruh." I cut Hasan off. Something inside me was telling me that Hasan wasn't cool. I don't know; I just didn't like his ass. "They call me Wah. It's good to meet you, my man." I stuck my hand out and offered it to him after setting the briefcase down in front of us. "This is Shug. That's Drape, and that's my man Camron." I introduced the crew.

"I see that you're a man who is about his business," Keitho spoke to me.

"That's what we here for, ain't it?"

"Exactly, son. Show me what you got, B."

"Wah. My name is Wah." I looked at Keitho hard, letting him know that he needed to address me by my name.

"Show me what you got, *Wah*." He spit my name out, chewing on the end of the blunt, mean-mugging me with his eyes.

I ignored his big burly ass for now and flipped the briefcase open.

He put his closed fist up to his mouth. "Whew wee! Nice, I like this shit right here. This is some fly shit, yo!"

"You ain't tellin' me nothin' I didn't know already. Can you cover the cost or not? Am I wasting my time here or what?"

He looked up at me and frowned hard. "What are you asking for all of this?"

"One point five million.'" I poured one of the bags of diamonds onto the table to reinforce my position.

"I think I can do that." He eyed the diamonds like a hungry hostage looking at a delicious plate of soul food.

"You think, or you can?" I wasn't trying to play around in this fool's neck of the woods. Seemed like he was a grimy type nigga for real.

He rubbed his chin in thought for a second. "I can do it. Let's meet back here tomorrow and make it happen."

"All da time. We'll slide back through tomorrow then." I stood up and gave him a pound, and then pulled him close to me. I patted him on the back and sealed the deal. Keitho was tagged now.

We left the building and split from Hasan.

When we got back to the hotel, we shut the door and pow-wow'd amongst each other.

"What made you tag his ass, Wah?" Shug asked me.

"I had a gut feelin', bruh, and went with it."

"Gut feeling?"

"Yeah, a gut feeling. Think about it, Shug. His fat ass was way too willing to just hand over 1.5 million when he ain't even appraised the merchandise properly. The only type of ma'fucka who get down like that is a grimy ma'fucka with a hidden agenda."

"True dat. True dat, bruh. I can't argue with you on that point."

The four of us fired up blunts and sat around the table and listened to the recording together.

ICE MIKE

Keitho: *Tell Hasan I said good lookin' out for turnin' me on to these lame ass Cali niggas. Give him the ten g's we agreed on, too. The shit in that briefcase is official.*

Deep voice thug: *Done deal, Keitho. How you figure on catchin' all four of 'em niggas slippin' though, son? They insisted on holding their heaters or it was a no deal.*

Keitho: *When they walk past the beaded curtain, I'ma hit the switch and seal they ass in there. You drop the gas on 'em, and as soon as they all dead, you vacuum that bitch out and the briefcase is all ours. It don't matter if they got guns or not."*

Deep voice thug: *What if they ask to see the money first?*

Keitho: *Then we show it to they asses, and then gas 'em. They gon' be a lot more relaxed and at ease if they're walkin' up outta here with all that money in hand. Once they're in the beaded room, we gas 'em on the way out.*

Deep voice Thug: *Fo' sho, fam'. I like how that sound, son. Comin' or goin', them clowns is gettin' gassed one way or the other!*

The grimy ass New York gangstas laughed at their evil scheme. I shut the recorder off and shook my head. For the rest of the night we went back and forth with different ideas and strategies.

Before the night was over, we had formulated a game plan that I felt would guarantee our success.

DEEPLY ROOTED

CHAPTER TWENTY-TWO
Pockets Heavier

Wahdatah

The next morning I woke up knowing that I was going to kill a man, so it didn't make any sense stressing on that fact. Instead, I focused my attention on the soft, warm naked flesh lying next to me.

I had felt Tocarra slither into bed sometime during the early hours of the morning. She had only been sleeping for about four hours when I woke her up with two fingers in her pussy. Tocarra lay on her stomach, asshole naked as my fingers pushed in deep and pulled out in slow motion.

Her gushy slit steadily became wetter as my fingers began to stroke her tightness faster. When I heard that lustful moan escape her lips, I knew she was ready to get broke off with this long, hard dick. I moved her to the middle of the king-size and nudged her thighs open wider with my knee as I positioned myself above her, my left hand flat on the bed next to her left ear for balance.

I gripped the shaft of my piece and stuck the head in. "Mmmm." She turned her head to the side and pushed that big, soft ass back at me. I pushed about three-inches up in her and stirred her hot honey pot with the end of my love muscle like her coochie was a jar of warm jelly. Her eyelashes fluttered and she moaned again. I thrust forward and the dick hit rock bottom after I stuffed it all the way up in her. I pulled it almost all the way out; then shoved it all the way back in again and started slow pounding the pussy, making sure I dipped back in from a different angle every time that I plunged into her wet, plush walls. Five minutes later, she cried out her joy.

"Ooh yes, Wah. Oh, hell yeah, baby! Get it just like that, daddy. Work that dick, baby!" She was on her knees now, legs wide open, ass tooted high in the air, trying to throw the pussy back at me.

I pounded harder, plunged deeper, and stroked faster. Still banging her back out from a different angle every time. Her pussy gripped my dick tighter, and her body shook hard with orgasm again. "Ugghh!" She came and her pussy flooded my pole with her sticky happiness. It only made me fuck her more frantically.

While her body bucked with her second orgasm, I grabbed a handful of her hair and wrapped it around my fist. I yanked her head back roughly and exposed her long, slender neck. The dick was still beating the pussy up relentlessly. I bit into her neck softly, and then sucked on it hard, banging away at her gushy like I was mad at the pussy.

"Oh yes, Wah. Please don't stop! Baby, you drivin' me fuckin' crazy!"

I pushed her face down into one of the soft fluffy pillows and used my other hand to grab hold of her hip. I threw the dick up in her with all the force I could muster; I was trying to stand up in the pussy!

"Ungh! Ungh! Ungh! Ungh!" I grunted loudly as I banged away at that thang. Smashing the shit out of her softness.

After twenty minutes of non-stop strokin', I felt my nuts swell up and explode. I busted a nut all over her ass and back. My breathing was heavy, heart racing with excited satisfaction. I fell on top of Tocarra, and laid my weight on her, feeling good about the quickie. I sucked on her earlobe and whispered, "Can you see yourself wakin' up to some of that every day?"

"Mm hmm, I sure can," she said breathlessly.

I rolled off her, lay on my back, and fired up a blunt. *My money was straight and our relationship was going in the right direction. Why not?* I thought. "Good, because when we get back to Cali I want you to find a nice four or five bedroom house for us, baby. I think it's time for us to take it to the next level."

"For real? Are you serious, Wah?" She turned to look at me with a surprised expression.

"As a heart attack." My eyes smiled at her.

"Okay then, that's what's up. Speaking of heart attacks." She smiled a naughty smile and climbed down between my legs and started licking and sucking on me until I was back on brick.

Tocarra repositioned herself after I was rock hard until we were in a sixty-nine position. I stuffed my entire tongue as deep as I could into her pussy—jabbed my tongue in and out of her parted lips as fast as my tongue would go. She squished her wet hotness down onto my face and grinded on my mouth, sliding the pussy back and forth over my lips. I grabbed both of her fleshy ass cheeks and took control of the situation. I lifted her ass up and spread her swollen lips open with my thumbs. I sucked up and swallowed all her pussy juice, and then flicked my tongue about wildly across her clitoris. She bucked hard and came again, releasing a thick stream of her girl cream into my mouth. I swallowed every bit of that too.

Tocarra slid down my body until her pussy was on top of my torso, I could feel her wet lips on my belly button. She turned to look into my eyes, and then reached around and grabbed hold of my thick hard-on. Easing her weight on it, she slid down my dick slowly. The pussy seemed hotter and wetter than before. She rode me with an aggressive passion in her hips. Her big chocolate brown-tipped titties swung in front of my face as she bounced hard on my meat. Her eyes locked onto my eyes, and she fucked on my dick like she was in charge of it. My toes curled and cracked like knuckles. I felt her pussy juice wash all over my dick and balls one more time. I couldn't help myself. I nutted again deep inside her hot wetness.

Tocarra got off the dick and went back down to suck it again. "Seriously?" I asked, exhausted. I was wore the fuck out.

"As a heart attack." She looked up at me and smiled before my dick disappeared.

That afternoon I spent most of the day with Tocarra, sightseeing, lunch, and a walk through Central Park. We took a few pictures in Times Squares and talked at length about our short-term and long-term goals, and seriously discussed the direction our relationship was going in.

I pulled Tocarra close and kissed her softly on the lips before I spoke. "Baby, you talk so freely about the future but I noticed that you're very guarded when you talk about your past. Why's that?"

ICE MIKE

She grew quiet and the glow on her face dimmed. Her eyes filled with sadness and then she tried to smile and front like it was all good. I wasn't buying it. Something about her past was haunting her.

"Talk to me, Tocarra. What is it?" I lifted her chin and made her look at me. She tried to turn her head but I wouldn't let her. Tears filled her pretty hazel eyes.

"I-I just." She froze up and got quiet again.

"What's up? Talk to me, ma. Whatever it is, I got you. I ain't goin' nowhere," I told her and meant it. Finally she let it out, the demon that had been haunting her for years.

"I can't have any children, Wah." She uttered the statement under her breath and cast her eyes down in shame.

The heaviness of what she just said forced a weighty silence between us. My heart broke for her. Her pain, unmistakable. Seeing her in pain like that hurt me deep.

"Come here, girl. Pick your chin up," I said and swallowed her up in a hug. "It's okay, baby. That don't change what we have, and it damn sure don't change how I feel about you." I assured her and held her tight.

Her voice was a whisper when she spoke. "Since we've met, so many times when we've talked you mentioned how badly you want to have kids and start a family one day. And I can't give you that. I've fallen in love with you, and I can't give the man I love the thing he desires most." We sat down and she told me her ovaries were severely compromised and the doctors told her that she would never be able to have children.

"Just because the doctors said it don't make it gospel, baby," I told her and tilted her chin up again. "Look at me.

Stop puttin' your head down, baby. You don't have nothin'
to be ashamed about."

She looked up at me and tears started flowing from her
eyes.

"That don't change nothin'. It don't change shit, ma. It
don't change the fact that you are a beautiful, intelligent,
strong-minded black woman! It don't change the fact that
you are a hard-working, educated, independent sistah who's
made somethin' out of her life despite being on your own
since you were sixteen! It don't change the fact that you are
a gifted writer who has written several successful novels!
And it damn sure don't change the fact that I love you, and
I'ma keep on lovin' you regardless."

"When you told me your pops ain't never really been in
your life and you left home at sixteen because your
mother's boyfriend forced himself on you, I understood
your pain. I know what it's like to grow up without a father.
I can only imagine how hard it was for you, baby. And
that's one of the reasons why I love you. Because you are a
survivor. Baby, we are survivors! You didn't let the bad shit
that happened in your past define your future. You're a
fighter and I admire you for that. Tocarra, I wish I could be
as straight-laced as you are. I wish I had it in me to live the
right way like you do."

My words hit her in the heart and made her look at me. I
wiped her tears away with my thumbs and kissed her on the
lips. I could tell by the look she gave me that she was
surprised that I remembered so many of the things she
revealed to me in past conversations, so I continued to
reinforce what it was I saw in her.

"Baby, you're smart, you're sexy, and you're ambitious. You got a cool personality and a bomb ass sense of humor that keeps me laughing. I dig everything about you, Tocarra, and the fact that you can't have kids don't change none of that, you feel me? Besides, that ain't gon' stop me from tryin' to put a baby in your fine ass. We gonna work on that every day!" I tucked her under my arm and we walked away from Times Square with a deeper bond than when we got there.

The more time we spent together, the more apparent it became to the both of us that we were good for each other. Our vibe flowed effortlessly; we were on the same page about a lot of the things that make a relationship go. I had more fun with Tocarra in one day than I had with most chicks in months.

We shared many of the same tastes; we both loved soul food. We loved the same type of music. She loved the thug life, loved writing about it. I loved living it. We both liked sports and were die hard Dallas Cowboys fans. The sex was incredible, and we got along so easily. But more than anything and most importantly, we accepted each other as is. She knew what I was about, and she fucked with me despite my flaws. I accepted her the same, cherished her perfections, and embraced what she perceived to be her biggest flaw.

* * * * *

Our plan was in motion. That night, all four of us were back in front of the heavy metal door with Hasan in front of us.

The metal slot slid open.

"What's your bizness?" The same blood shot eyes stared at us as last time.

"Keitho is expectin' us," Hasan spoke for everybody.

The sound of the heavy metal door unlocking reminded me of prison. I thought about my father, and wondered what it must've been like for him to do twenty-three years in a concrete cage, and then finally realize that he would never get the chance to spend any of the millions that he had killed a man for.

He stepped up to search us again.

"We been through this shit before, bruh. We ain't partin' with our bangers. Go get ya' boss and let's do this same song and dance, playboy. If y'all got guns, then we gon' have guns!" Me and the crew posted like statues and let it be known we weren't budging on the issue.

"Wait here," he told us. Dude didn't seem as upset as the last time. He left and came back two minutes later wearing a smile.

"Follow me, fam'," the deep-voiced thug said.

I kept my hand on the chrome, ready to bust. We walked with him a few steps and then I abruptly stopped.

"Say, bruh. Tell ya man Keitho that I wanna see some dough first. No dough, no deal." I made sure we stopped before we got to the beaded curtain. I could see the opening running up and down the length of the doorway where the sliding door was hidden. I tried to locate the gas holes, but I couldn't see anything.

"Wait right here," the deep-voiced thug said again.

He showed up with Keitho next to him a couple minutes later. "What's the problem, son? Why all the hostility?"

ICE MIKE

"I wanna see some cheese before we deal, folks." My hand was wrapped around the fo'-five in my hoodie pocket. "Ain't nothin' hostile about that, bruh."

"Ai'ight, that's cool. Walk with me," Keitho said and turned.

I followed with Drape on my heels.

Once we got in the back office he stopped. "Post up, duke," Keitho said. He went over to a safe on the wall.

The safe clicked open, and I saw a grip of money stacks. At least a million and half reasons to set it off.

Doom! Doom!

The fo'-five roared, and Keitho took two in the back. He slumped to the floor, twisted in anguish. Dead.

Kak! Kak! Kak!

Drape's nine popped off shots. The deep-voiced thug was on his back, shaking in the throes of death.

Pop! Pop! Pop!

The doorman with the bloodshot eyes was sitting on his back pockets motionless. Three holes in his chest. Shug was vicious with the pistol.

"What the fuck y'all do that for?" Hasan asked. He was hella shook up. All the bitch in him was on full display.

"I thought you was good people, Hasan." Shug looked the traitorous New York busta in his eyes before he bapped him with an expert double-tap.

Pop! Pop!

Both shots hit Hasan in the face. He fell backward to the floor and pooted before he expired.

DEEPLY ROOTED

When we touched back down in San Diego, our pockets were a million and a half dollars heavier, and I still had the briefcase full of stolen jewelry and diamonds.

Part III

DEEPLY ROOTED

CHAPTER TWENTY-THREE
Revenge

Jracia

J ust when she thought mercy had smiled on her, while on the brink of a much needed sleep, the incessant vibrating started again. Jracia put her head under the pillow and tried her damnedest to ignore the continuous humming noise coming from the vibrating phone on the bedside table. She peeked through a teary eye up at the clock and let out an exasperated breath of disgust when she saw that it read 6:02 AM.

"Aaahhhggghhhh!" An angry scream of disappointment jumped from her throat. "Hello!" Her greeting was rude and blunt.

"Is this Jracia?" the soft voice inquisitively asked on the other end.

"Who the fuck is this? And why the fuck are you calling my phone early in the fuckin' morning like this!"

"Is this Jracia?" the soft voice repeated the question evenly.

"Bitch, I ain't got time for this! If I find out who the fuck you are, I'ma beat yo' ass!"

"Don't you wanna know who killed your man Wicked?"

"What!" The question caught Jracia off guard. It shook her out of her sleepy state and woke her up with wide-eyed confusion. The words knocked her off her pivot and nudged her brain off-balance. The mention of Wicked's name had her wide awake now.

"I said, don't you want to know who murdered your man?" The soft voice had a little bit of sass in it now, recognizing that her words were having the desired effect.

"Whatchu' know about what happened to Wicked?"

"I know who pulled the trigger." The soft voice teased Jracia's desire to know by dropping that lug in her lap.

"Who?"

"Wouldn't you like to know?"

Click.

"Hello? Hello!" Jracia started to panic when she realized the caller had disconnected. She looked at the screen on her phone in an attempt to identify who had just called her and further fucked up her already frazzled state of mind. The call was from a restricted number.

Jracia threw the comforter and sheets off her and ran to the bathroom. The light skinned, green-eyed beauty barely made it to the toilet when she threw-up into the bowl. She hugged the rim of the toilet and spat out the foul taste in her mouth.

It had all started a month after Wicked was gunned down. The bouts of morning sickness. Her little friend had not come to see her this month either. She had been pregnant before and recognized the signs.

After rinsing her mouth out, she cleaned up around the toilet and reached for the pregnancy test she had bought on the way home the other day. She peed on the stick, and set it on the box that rested on top of a pile of unraveled tissue paper.

ICE MIKE

Jracia sat on the edge of the bathtub and closed her eyes. A small part of her hoped that she was not pregnant. The thought of being a single mother terrified the nineteen year old. The possibility of raising a child by herself because the father was dead made her shrink away from the thought of it. But she had fallen deeply in love with the handsome thug whom she had met just over a year ago. Her mind flashed back to the time when her best friend Tatiana had hooked them up. At first, she had been a little skeptical, hesitant to allow her feelings to get seriously involved with a man in prison because she had heard so many heartbreaking horror stories that some of her home girls had experienced. Falling for a man in prison, and then taking care of that man by doing the time with him. Letters, pictures, phone calls, packages, and being finger-fucked in the visiting room. Doing all of that, only to have that same man get out and shake you like dice. Jracia was tentative with her emotions initially, but as what usually applies with affairs of the heart, her hesitancy gave way to the undeniable. She fell in love with Wicked, and was simply left to hope that hers too would not become another one of those heartbreaking horror stories.

Her belief in true love was rewarded when Wicked was finally released from prison, and not only did he come home to her, he moved in with her and held her household down for the few weeks he had been out. He regularly broke her off large sums of money, and he kept a hard dick deep up in her on a daily basis. It was the first time in her young life that a thug had treated her like a lady and fucked her like a porn star while always keeping it one hundred.

DEEPLY ROOTED

Jracia was still in love with Wicked, and that love for him strongly entertained thoughts of having his baby, and raising their child by herself if she had to.

She looked up from where she sat and tears rolled down her face dropping off her chin and falling onto her lap. Thoughts of a love lost so tragically tormented her heart with pain. Jracia hurt deep down inside to her core. When she saw the pregnancy test confirm what she had already known, she walked from the bathroom in a daze. She fell across the bed where she and Wicked had shared so many beautiful, lustful moments—not enough of them as far as she was concerned. Her frame shook with sorrow from the thought of her man being brutally gunned down in her car. The thought of her one true love being taken away from her so violently, made her want to kill whoever was responsible for his death.

Her phone vibrating on the top of her bedside table snatched her from the depths of despair. Jracia had drifted off to a painful place. The call was from a restricted number.

"Hello?" she said hopefully.

"If you want to know who killed your man, go to your front door and look inside that envelope. The answers to all of your questions are right there." The soft voice had a sinister undertone to it.

Forgetting about her morning sickness, Jracia threw on some sweats, snatched her hair up into a ponytail, and went to the living room. She eyeballed the peephole in the center of her door, and then peeked out the corner of one of her living room curtains in hopes of catching a glimpse of whoever it was that kept calling. She saw nothing.

ICE MIKE

She opened the front door not knowing what to expect. On the ground at her feet was a large manila envelope. It was bulky and ominous looking. She was afraid to pick it up. Jracia peered into the street again, but saw nothing out of the ordinary. A sucked up crackhead dragging his heavy, sleep deprived feet in search of another hit. The old, gray-haired woman, Mrs. Rose was across the street watering a small patch of green grass surrounded by concrete and dirt that looked out of place on the block. A wolf pack of nappy-headed, loud mouth young boys up to no good, were throwing rocks at passing cars.

Again, she looked down at the package at her feet. Finally, she bent down and picked it up, holding it away from her body like it was a ticking time bomb. She closed the door and switched her hips hard over to the coffee table. *This thing is hella heavy!* she thought, weighing the envelope in her hand before setting it down. It hit the table with a thud. She picked at the flattened metal clasps and peeled the envelope open. The first thing that caught her eyes was the huge hand-canon at the bottom of the envelope.

The chrome .357 Magnum looked menacing. Then her eyes were drawn to the glossy 8 x 10 picture inside.

Jracia pulled the photograph out and examined it closely. It was a photo of four well-dressed, handsome looking thugs. In the background, the beautiful New York skyline exhibited skyscrapers and snow falling softly to the ground. Of the four faces, two of them had red circles around them.

Jracia studied the circled faces intensely. She turned the photograph over and looked at the back of it. There were two addresses scribbled neatly at the top. Under it was a note. Her heart raced with adrenaline as she read it:

DEEPLY ROOTED

The two men who pulled the trigger and killed your boyfriend are circled. I put their addresses at the top in the event that you decide to do the right thing. Just so you know, it was a case of mistaken identity. Your man died for nothing, simply because he looked like somebody else.

What is my stake in all of this you might ask! Let's just say that I was there when it happened, and it was fucked up the way that they gunned your man down in cold blood. I want justice served, but this isn't my beef. It's yours. He was your man, so it is your obligation.

Good luck with that . . .

The letter wasn't signed. To her it didn't make any sense. Jracia felt the need for revenge coursing through her veins. She picked the pistol up and examined it closely after she sat the envelope on the table. She held the heavy handgun in her hands and closed her eyes. Visions of Wicked played like a silent film behind her closed eyelids. Their very first kiss. The day he got out of prison. The last time he dicked her down, how gangsta his deep stroke was. She wondered how he would've reacted to the news of her pregnancy. Him holding her in his strong arms making her feel so safe. That last image tipped her over the edge. A single tear slowly crawled down her cheek and fell on her hand, the hand that cradled the huge pistol tightly. That's all it took; her mind was made up. Jracia needed to do the right thing.

* * * * *

Ready to go to war, Jracia whipped Wicked's white Cutlass all the way across town until she was at one of the addresses on the back of the photo.

Knock. Knock. Knock. Knock. Knock.

A minute later, the door opened and Tupac's "Hail Mary" beat loudly in the background.

Jracia immediately recognized him as one of the men whose face was circled on the photo.

"What's good, ma? How can I help you?" He eyed her luscious body lustfully. *Damn this bitch is raw as fuck and she thick as hell too!* He eye-fucked Jracia openly.

"You can't do shit for me, you son of a bitch!" the green-eyed beauty responded with hatred written all over her face.

"Then what the fuck is you here for, 'ho?" He said angrily, put off by her shitty attitude.

"I'm here for Wicked."

"What! Bitch, ain't no Wicked here."

Boom!

The .357 barked loud and bucked hard in her hand. The slug hit him in the chest and staggered him. He landed hard on his back pockets and clutched at his chest. With wide eyes, he struggled desperately to ask her why she shot him.

Jracia stepped inside the doorway and pointed the pistol at him.

Boom!

He tried to ask the question again.

Boom!

The last bullet punched a hole in his head and knocked him out forever.

Minutes later, the Cutlass rolled slowly down a different block. Jracia's eyes searched for the second address that matched the one on the back of the 8 x 10. She parked the Cutlass and jumped out after finding it.

Ding! Dong! Ding!

DEEPLY ROOTED

The doorbell chimed loudly.

When the door opened, she recognized the second face that was circled on the photograph.

"What's up wit' it?" He answered the door in some baggy jeans and a wife beater.

Boom! Boom! Boom!

This time Jracia wasted no time. Her first murder gave her the confidence to pull the trigger. It also made her realize that she didn't have the luxury of playing word games, or acting it out like a movie script. She left the door open, his body on the floor gasping for air, air that seemed harder and harder to come by. As she fled the scene she heard a woman scream behind her.

Twenty-minutes later, when Jracia opened the door to her crib, she breathed a sigh of relief. Filled with a feeling of accomplishment, she kicked off her shoes and started stripping out of her outfit. She wanted to take a shower. Wash off the stench of death that was on her.

Pop!

A bullet ripped into Jracia's back and settled near her belly button after tearing through her intestines. She grabbed at her back, then her stomach. She knew that the life that had just started growing inside of her was dead.

Pop! Pop!

Two more bullets hit her in the heart from the back, and she died much like she had started the day: on her knees with her head in the toilet.

CHAPTER TWENTY-FOUR
What's Really Going On?

Shug

Hey you! What's up, sleepy head?" Miko asked Shug when he walked into the kitchen.

"Mornin', babe." He dipped his head and kissed his woman. "It smells good as hell up in here. Whatchu cookin', ma?" He pulled the blue Seattle Mariners fitted cap down low on his head and turned it slightly to the left. The crisp white tee, Coogi denim shorts, and white Air Force Ones was his choice of outfit for the day. His wrist, neck, and ears were blinged out. "How long you been up, baby?"

"Pancakes, scrambled eggs, bacon, toast, and juice." She set a plate down in front of him. "I got a gift for you too, baby." Her lips touched his ear when she said it. "Paid top dollar for it, daddy." Miko answered his first question and skirted around his second question.

"Is that right? Whatchu' get me, girl?"

"Here." She handed him a square box.

He shook it. No clue. Shug tore the gift-wrap paper off and admired the highly polished expensive wood box. He twisted the clasp on it and whistled his appreciation at the magnificent chrome pistol nestled in the velvet lining.

"This ma'fucka is pretty as fuck, baby!" He kissed her and thanked her and then excused himself from the table. "I'll be back in a sec, ma."

Miko was glad that Shug liked the gift. He had to get rid of his other strap in New York, so she purchased another one. He didn't tell her why, or what had happened, but she had been with him long enough to know when he had done some grimy shit. During those times, Shug wouldn't fuck her hard. Instead, he would patiently make the most passionate and tender love to her. The night before they left New York, he had taken her somewhere sexually that she had never been before. His lovemaking that night had been incredibly patient, and sensuously tender to a point where she wanted to shed tears. When he released himself in her that night, she knew without a doubt that he had killed somebody. She smiled at the memory just as he made his way back into the kitchen.

"Baby, we've been doing this thing together for a while now, and from day one you've been everything that I could've ever wished for in a woman. You stood by my side and didn't flinch an inch when times got tough. Baby, you are who I see when I close my eyes and visualize who it is that I want to spend the rest of my life with. Miko, will you marry me?" He was on one knee with the biggest diamond ring that she had ever seen. No shame in his game, he was in love and loved the fact that he was.

She gushed with happiness. "Yes! Yes, I'll marry you, baby." Miko was near tears. They kissed, and he held her in his arms tightly.

Eventually they sat down to eat. The conversation was non-stop and flowed easy between them. It always had.

"Where's your brother, baby?"

"I don't know. He said that he was gonna hit me up, but I ain't heard from him all day."

"Oh yeah, that's right. I think I heard Tocarra mention something about the two of them going house hunting soon." Miko remembered.

"He'll be through later on. He knows that we supposed to meet up later to take care of some business, so I'm sure he'll slide through. If he ain't showed up by five, then I'll hit him up and see what's good."

"Yeah, because we really do need to sit down and focus our energy on making some serious business decisions. Figure out the best ways in which to invest some of this money. You feel me?" Miko asserted herself.

"Look at you, actin' all CEO and shit." Shug clowned with her.

"You laughin', baby, but I'm serious as hell. That's the only way that we're going to get up out of these streets and get on some real boss shit. You know what I'm sayin'?"

"I know, baby girl. You're right. Me and Wah been puttin' our heads together and comin' up with some plans. He got some good ideas too."

"What about Cam? Y'all holler today?"

"Naw. As a matter of fact we haven't, but it's still early though. You know that horny nigga probably somewhere fuckin' up in Monisha right now."

She took his plate when he finished and put it in the sink and then walked up behind him. "You know what? I feel like whoopin' your ass in somethin', daddy!" Miko challenged her fiancé, her pelvis pressing up against his back.

"What! You know you ain't tryin' to see me at nothin', Miko!" His competitive juices were activated now. "How you want it, ma?" He was ready for whatever. "What, X-Box? PlayStation? Strip poker? Tell daddy how you want it, Miko?"

"Well, since you got yourself that new gun and all, I figure we can have a shoot-out and shoot some shit up!" Miko's competitive juices were flowing too.

"You ain't said nothin' but a word, mama."

"Three shots apiece. Most hits win, and we playin' for blow jobs, baby!" She smiled when she winked at him.

"You must really just wanna suck on a dick, huh? Shit, all you gotta do is ask, baby. I ain't got no problem puttin' this meat in ya mouth."

"Fuck you, Shug. Let's go. It's kinda chilly outside this morning, so I'ma put a hoodie on, and if I gotta wear one, then you gotta wear one too."

"However you wanna do it, baby girl. I can do this shit butt-naked, or in a space suit. It don't matter to me. You know I ain't gon' let no girl beat me." He laughed.

Miko playfully flipped him off and left the room before coming back seconds later with her .380 and his powder blue San Diego Charger hoodie in her hand. She was wearing her pink Baby Phat hoodie.

"Here." She tossed him his.

He pulled the hoodie over his head and took the pistol out of the wooden box. "Let's go do this then." He had his game face on.

They lined up a six-pack of soda cans on the three-foot high wall in the backyard. It wasn't the first time they had done this.

"Do you wanna take your shots from up here, baby?" He wore a serious expression on his face when he extended his offer to allow her to cheat.

"I see you got jokes, huh? Hell naw. I don't need no help." She refused his offer to shoot from ten feet closer.

"Okay then, being the gentleman that I am, ladies first." He bowed and let her shoot first.

Miko raised the .380 and aimed it. She took a deep breath and exhaled softly before squeezing the trigger.

Pop!

The soda can furthest to the left exploded.

"Nice shot. Luck perhaps?" He taunted her, and then raised the chrome and shot.

Boom!

His pistol roared, and the can in the middle disappeared.

"Talk about luck." She razzed him back and prepared for her second shot.

Pop!

The soda can on the far right end vanished.

"I like to cover all the bases when I shoot, from A to Z. You feel me?" She laughed and stepped aside so he could shoot.

Boom!

Once again the soda can in the middle burst open and fell over.

"I like to be consistent with mines, *you feel me*?" he remarked mockingly and winked at her.

"Smart ass."

Miko took her position and raised the .380.

Shug stepped up close to her and whispered against her ear. "They say that pressure bust a pipe, but I'm sure that that's just a myth, huh?" he teased.

She smiled, and then took a deep breath before slowly releasing it.

Pop!

The dirt on the hill behind the wall moved. A small cloud of dust appeared, and then disappeared.

"Uh oh. I guess it is true, baby. Pressure do bust pipes," he clowned and bent in half with laughter.

"Your turn, asshole!" Miko was no doubt a sore loser.

Baby Shug lifted his pistol and squeezed one of his eyes shut. "Start gettin' that jaw loosened up, baby. I'ma be needin' that blow job before company gets here." He was cocky to say the least.

Boom!

The can directly in front of him blew up. "It's all in the wrist bab—"

"Fuck you, Shug!" She stormed off and walked into the house steaming hot.

Fifteen minutes later, Miko swallowed the hot nut that splashed against the back of her neck.

"I'm still shootin' and consistently hittin' the middle, ma, huh?" he joked.

Knock. Knock. Knock.

ICE MIKE

Someone knocking at the door interrupted them.

"Will you get that please, baby, while I go brush my teeth?" she asked him.

"Ai'ight," he said, zipping up his shorts as he headed to the door.

Shug looked through the peephole and smiled at the pretty face in front of him. *Wahdatah had chosen well*, he thought as he twisted the doorknob.

"What's up, bruh?" He embraced Wahdatah and then gave Tocarra a hug.

"Where's Miko?" Tocarra quizzed.

"She'll be out in a minute. How'd it go with the house hunting?" he asked his brother.

"It went good, bruh. I think we settled on a nice five-bedroom joint out in the Del Mar area."

"Hey girl!" Tocarra and Miko hugged each other when she came out.

"So what's up, girl? How did it go?"

"It went great! We found a five-bedroom, six-bathroom two-story out in Del Mar that is so beautiful!"

The two women chatted away in excited conversation. Shug waited a couple of minutes before he hit them with the news of their engagement.

"Come here, baby." Shug motioned to Miko and took her by the hand. He pulled her close to his side. "I just wanted to share the moment with you and your girl, bruh. Over the past few months a lot has happened in our lives. I gained a brother and lost an enemy at the same time." He looked at Wahdatah and winked his eye. "I lost a grandmother and a father whom I had never had the pleasure of meeting before.

2 1 0

Through it all though, and long before any of that, this woman right here has been by my side." He kissed Miko on the forehead before going on. "That's why today I asked her to remain by my side for the rest of my life. I asked Miko to marry me." He was cheesing when he finished speaking.

Wahdatah smiled and pounded Shug. The two brothers hugged tightly.

"Congratulations, Shug. On the real, bruh. I'm hella happy for you."

"Girl, let me see that rock!" Tocarra inspected the huge diamond on Miko's hand.

Ring. Ring. Ring.

They had been talking for twenty minutes when Shug's phone sounded off. "Yeah dat?" he answered.

"Shug, this is Monisha. Camron is dead. Somebody killed my baby!"

"What! Don't play with me, Mo. On mommas, Mo. Don't fuck with me like that!" Shug stood up waiting for her response, hoping she was bullshitting. But deep down inside, he knew she wasn't, because the dread in her voice was all too real.

Everybody in the room was as silent as death.

"He's dead, Shug! I was right here at the house when it happened. They just put him in a bag!"

"Don't go nowhere. I'm on my way!" He grabbed his keys and the pistol Miko had just given him as a gift. "That was Monisha. Somebody killed Camron!"

"What!" Everybody in the room exclaimed at the same time in shocked surprise.

Shug was emotionally rocked. Camron had been his best friend since childhood. He tried to focus on his thoughts, but everything was a blur in his head.

"C'mon, Miko. Y'all rollin' wit' us?" he asked Wahdatah and Tocarra.

"Hell yeah, let's go," Wahdatah spoke for the both of them.

Two minutes later, Shug closed the door behind them.

Wahdatah and Tocarra were right behind them in his Charger when Wahdatah's phone began to ring.

"Whaddup?" he answered.

"Is this Wahdatah?" a female voice asked on the other end of the line.

"Who the fuck is this?" he growled his own question back.

"It's Carmelita—"

"Bitch, why the fuck is you callin' my phone?" He smashed on the hood rat before she could finish speaking.

"It's Drape. I—"

"What about Drape?" Something in her voice warned him of a bad thing.

"He's dead. Somebody shot him!"

"I'ma kill you if you lyin', bitch!" he threatened. Then he hung up on her and yanked out the fo'-five. He racked the Desert Eagle, making sure it was ready to kill somebody. He wondered why Carmelita had called rather than Drape's new chick, Petra. He twisted the steering wheel, expertly negotiating a sharp right turn right behind Shug's Escalade. Wahdatah looked over at Tocarra, and she knew something was terribly wrong. He thumbed his cell phone.

"What's up, Wah?" Shug answered, sounding distraught.

"Drape just got knocked down, bruh! A bitch he used to fuck with just hit me up. She said somebody shot and killed Drape." He screwed his face up at the thought of how things were playing out. "Bruh, watch your back. It ain't no coincidence that both of our right hands got slumped around the same time."

"Who you think is behind this shit?" Shug posed the question.

"I can't even call it, bruh. It ain't no tellin', but if you look at everything that we had our hands in, it could be anybody. The Sicilian ma'fucka Joey Cheese's people, or them New York niggas wantin' some get-back. Man, I don't know!"

"Go 'head and see what it do with Drape. I'ma go check on Monisha and see what happened to Camron."

"Fo' sho'. Holla at me if you hear something, bruh."

"You too. Get at me if you find out anything, or just feel some kinda way about something," Shug responded before disconnecting.

Both couples went their separate ways, each car full of worry and revenge. Both brothers wheeling their whips and wondering what the hell was really going on.

CHAPTER TWENTY-FIVE
Bitch in a White Cutlass

Wahdatah

W hen I rolled down Drape's block, they had already taken his body away in the meat wagon. They said he was dead when the po-po showed up.

"C'mon, baby. Walk with me up here to his apartment. I want to see if there's anything there that will reveal something to me," I told Tocarra.

"I'm scared, Wah. I don't want anything to happen to you, baby. It would kill me if something were to happen to you." Tocarra held my arm close to her body. She was speaking from the heart.

"Don't be thinkin' like that, ma. Ain't nothin' finna happen to me. I promise I'ma always be here for you." I stopped at the bottom of the steps that led up to Drape's crib. I cupped her chin in my hand and kissed her softly on the lips. "I got you, Tocarra. Don't worry about me, okay?" Her eyes teared up when she smiled back at me. I knew she wasn't convinced by my words. She was just a good girl caught up in a bad boy's world. She was terrified, and I didn't like seeing her that way.

"Wah, they killed him!" she said it quietly, but it got my attention.

"I know, baby. I know." I pulled her close and held her. Every part of me wanted to shelter and protect this beautiful black woman.

Drape being dead made me start to think about other options in my life. My money was straight. I could take the money I had and bounce up out of San Diego on the next thang smoking. Maybe relocate somewhere back east, or down south in the ATL.

"I love you, Wahdatah, and I don't want anything to happen to you, baby." Tocarra clung to me tightly. I kissed her on the nose, and then on the lips.

"I gotchu', baby. I ain't goin' nowhere no time soon. Come here." I kissed her hard on the mouth to let her know I meant every word. I took her by the hand and led her up the stairs. Once I approached Drape's neighbor's door, I knocked three times. The yellow crime scene tape and the sealed apartment door made it painfully clear that my closest homeboy, Drape wasn't ever coming back. In a few short months, I had literally lost a handful of people closest to my heart. Family and close friends who I truly loved and cared for.

"What's good, Silky?" I said when the young, dark complexioned sistah opened the door.

"Hey, Wah. How you doin'?" Her eyes were red and swollen. Drape had been fucking Silky on the side, but she was the homie Moolah's little sister, so they had to keep it on the low. Moolah may have been dead, but her other brothers were alive, and they would've flipped the fuck out if they knew that Drape was smashin' that.

"It's gon' be all right, Silky." I hugged the home girl and walked in. "This my girl Tocarra. Tocarra, this my home girl Silky."

"Nice to meet you." They hugged.

"I think it was a bitch that shot him, Wah," Silky said out of nowhere.

"Why you say that?" She had my undivided attention now.

"I was in the shower when I heard the first shot. I didn't know if it was a gunshot or what, so I waited until I heard a second shot. And then I heard another shot. I jumped outta the shower and ran to the window because the sound was so loud I knew it had to be close by. I saw a light-skinned bitch at the bottom of the stairs walkin' away hella fast. I stepped out and looked over the railing, and I saw her get inside a white Cutlass before she drove off."

"Did you say anything to the police?"

"Hell naw! I don't get down like that!"

"I didn't mean it like that, Silky. Do the po-po know anything about the white Cutty?"

"I don't even know. They talked to everybody, but wasn't nobody talkin' to them."

"What the bitch look like? Did you get a good look?" I needed a clue. Light-skinned bitch in a white Cutlass might not be enough.

"Nope. Just a thick, high-yellow chick in a white Cutlass."

We chopped it up for a few more minutes before I decided to shake the spot.

"Are you going to be all right?" I asked Silky after I stood up, ready to leave.

"Yeah, I'ma be okay, Wah. Thanks. It's just gonna be hard. First Moo and Thun-Thun, now Drape . . ." Her voice trailed off, full of sadness.

"Hit me up if you need anything, Silk. You know I gotchu', lil mama." I hugged her and kissed her on the forehead before I turned to leave. Tocarra hugged her too, and I closed the door behind us.

As soon as I sat down in the Charger, I picked up the cell phone and called my brother.

"What up wit' it?" he answered.

"Ain't nothin'. What's good?" I responded.

"It's all bad, bruh. They hit Cam wit' three to the chest. He was dead when them people showed up."

I explained to him the same thing had happened to Drape.

"This ain't no coincidence, Shug. You know that, right?" I told him.

"I feel you, Wah. It damn sho' ain't no coincidence. One of the neighbors said they saw a white Cutlass push off the curb after Cam got clacked on."

"A light-skinned bitch?" I asked him.

"Yeah, how you know?"

"One of Drape's neighbor's saw the same thing."

"It don't make no sense, Wah. A bitch? It gotta be a connection, something we ain't seein'."

"If it ain't that, then that bitch was a hired hitter, Shug."

"Yeah dat. I was thinkin' the same thing."

"So that's what it is then."

"Yes sir, and it's shoot on sight, dawg."

"I'ma drop Tocarra off and then go holla at some of the homies. See if anybody know anything."

"I'ma do the same. Hit me back if you stumble up on something."

"All da time, bruh."

"Gone."

"One."

I put my phone up and turned to Tocarra. She turned away and looked out the window.

"Don't be like that, ma." I reached across the console and stroked her thigh affectionately.

She didn't respond.

"If it was you who got killed, I would be doing the same thing, Tocarra. This was my boy. I grew up with Drape, baby. He was like a brother to me."

"I just don't want nothing bad to happen to you." Her eyes filled with tears.

"Ain't nothing bad gonna happen to me, baby."

When the car stopped in front of the crib, she leaned over and kissed me passionately. We savored the sweet kiss, taking turns sucking on one another's bottom lip before finally separating. We got out of the car, and I walked her to the front door.

"I'll be back through later, okay?"

"I meant it when I said that I love you, Wah."

"C'mere." I squeezed her soft ass cheeks and pressed up against her. "I love you too, Tocarra." I kissed her again and felt her melt in my arms. Shit, I was melting in her arms as well.

"Be safe, baby."

"All da time, ma."

In seconds I was pushing the whip hard, banging Pac's "All Eyez On Me" with the fo'-five in my lap. My mind was working overtime trying to figure this shit out. *Who the fuck was behind these murders? Was it Joey Cheese's people? Was it the New York nigga, Keitho's people? It can't be about that fool in the Camry. Drape and Camron didn't have shit to do with that.* I continued to mash on the gas and push the bully whip in and out of traffic. I made a few stops and talked to a few people. By the time I got back to my crib, I still had more questions than I did answers. My mind was a complete blank with the exception of one image running around in my head—a light-skinned bitch in a white Cutlass.

CHAPTER TWENTY-SIX
A Necessary Distraction

Baby Shug

W hen Shug and Miko returned home, he headed straight to the shower and tried to rinse away the foul reality that was upon him. His boy Camron was dead, murdered by a bitch. It wasn't making any sense to him, but they had been murking people for years together. *Maybe it was revenge for one of the many ma'fuckas we put down in the past.* Thoughts kept popping up in his head, while the answers to those thoughts remained hidden.

Miko hung up the phone just as Shug walked into the bedroom butt-naked, water dripping down his brown skin, causing his heavily tattooed frame to shine with wetness.

"We're gonna get to the bottom of this, baby," Miko assured him and grabbed up a towel. She began to pat his body until he was dry. Then she hit his skin with some scented lotion. She could feel the tension in his muscles as she rubbed him down.

"I just wanna find out who did this so I can snatch they ass up and kill 'em slow. I don't give a fuck what it takes. I won't rest until I find the bitch responsible and murk her ass!" His anger was evident; the pain from his loss was etched into every line on his face. Spontaneous sex was a necessary distraction.

So he didn't resist when Miko dropped to her knees and took his limp meat into her mouth. She swallowed his dick and felt it grow big and hard on her tongue. His dickhead rubbed up against the back of her throat. The feeling of his massiveness excited her. She was soaking wet between the legs. The loud slurping sounds made Shug harden up with the quickness. He put his hands on her ears and held them. The hot, wet head was driving him crazy. It wasn't long before he was thrusting his erection in and out of her esophagus, trying his damnedest to choke her out.

Ten minutes later, Miko's fire head had him ready to explode.

"I'm finna cum, baby! I'm 'bout to nut. Aagghhh!" Shug pulled his dick out and shot thick spurts of hot cum in her face. Miko licked up whatever her tongue could touch. She let the rest run down her face, off her chin.

"Fuck me hard, baby. Now!" she insisted, pulling her pants down, climbing onto the bed tooting her ass in the air.

Shug looked at the irresistible vision of her wet, slick, camel-toe, and his love muscle flexed hard with desire. He stuck a finger in and poked her pussy perfectly.

"Oooh shit, baby. That feels good, but I need to feel that big dick up in me!" His swipe throbbed with pride, but he wanted to taste and tease her wet delight.

Shug fell to his knees and tongued her gooey slit. He probed her pink with his tongue and fingered her clit furiously. His dick grew rock hard in the process and he feasted on her pussy like it was his last meal. He tortured her pussy with his mouth for a few more minutes until Miko nutted in his mouth. Shug stood and roughly slapped the dick against her pussy lips, and then he stuck it in her slow, teasing her dripping wet pussy as he pulled half out.

"Yes, daddy! Stick it all the way in me please!" she begged him.

Shug jammed his dick in with savage force, and then started banging her hard and deep with lightning fast jackhammer strokes.

"Ungh! Ungh! Ungh! Oh, fuck yeah, daddy. Beat this pussy up!" Miko cried out with cum still all over her face.

Boom!

A loud crash made Shug snatch his dick out the pussy and reach for his pistol. He scurried into a pair of boxers. Miko wiped the thick cum that coated her face with the back of her hand and then crawled off the bed.

"Grab yo' gun, baby!" he yelled to Miko and gripped his new pistol tightly.

"San Diego Police Department!" several loud voices yelled from the front room.

The activity in the living room sounded like a stampede.

When Shug saw the uniformed police officers, all white cops, he tried to toss the pistol in the bedroom closet.

"Freeze! Put your motherfucking hands where I can see them before I shoot you!"

Moments later, Shug was sitting in the back of a police cruiser discombobulated. "Call my brother, Miko, and get me a lawyer, baby!" he yelled through the window.

She assured him that she would handle her business.

Miko cooperated with the police and handed over the chrome .357 she had given him, the gun that Shug had tossed. She also handed the police officer the powder blue

San Diego Charger hoodie as well; it had gun residue on it just as she had planned it. She went outside and walked up to the car where her man sat handcuffed in the backseat. "I love you," she mouthed to him. "I'll call Wah and find a good lawyer."

"Okay, I love you, too," he mouthed the words back.

Minutes later, he was being driven downtown facing multiple murder charges. The evidence against him was damning.

Miko went back inside and tried to clean up the mess the police had made when they bum-rushed her crib. The door was completely destroyed. There was no way she could stay there under those conditions. She called Monisha.

"They just took Shug to jail, and they fucked my house up in the process. I'm comin' to stay with you, okay?" She was already carrying one of her suitcases.

"What the hell did they take him to jail for?" Monisha asked, her thoughts momentarily off the tragedy in her life.

"Murder," Miko stated dryly.

"Murder! Who they tryin' to say he killed?"

"Camron and Drape," Miko replied.

"Who? What did you just say?" Monisha was dumbfounded.

"Girl, the police trying to say that Shug killed Camron and Drape. They took a gun and a hoodie as evidence."

"That's bullshit though, Miko! Shug would never do anything to hurt Camron!" Monisha knew in her heart that Shug loved Cam like a brother, and would never do anything to harm him. He damn sure wouldn't kill him.

ICE MIKE

"That's exactly what I said, Mo. Besides, Shug been over here at the house with me since we came back from New York." Miko was lugging the suitcase to her car. She had packed it while Shug was taking his shower. "I'll talk to you when I get there, okay, girl?"

"But . . . somethin' ain't right. This gotta be a setup. We gotta do something, Miko. We can't just sit back and let—"

Miko hung up without saying another word.

* * * * *

Shug sat handcuffed in the backseat, racking his brain and trying to figure out what the hell had just happened. One minute he was knee deep in some good pussy, stroking it with pleasure. The next minute he was hemmed up in some handcuffs in the back of a cop car charged with killing his closest friend and his brother's home boy. He couldn't wrap his mind around the shit going on around him. *I need to holla at Wah,* he thought as the patrol car pulled up next to the county jail intake door.

Just like every other inmate who came through the county jail, Shug was forced to endure the humiliating intake process—strip down ass-hole naked, lift your nut sac, bend over, spread your cheeks, and cough three times while another grown ass man visually inspected your asshole for contraband.

When Shug stepped into the fish tank, he had to breathe through his mouth until his system adjusted to the rank ass odor that permeated in the air like a thick cloud of invisible hot funk. The combination of bad breath, foul feet, stank armpits, and ass was violent to the nostrils and sinuses. His eyes watered up as a result of the sour odor. After five minutes of standing with his back against the wall observing the other people inside the holding tank, a youngster approached him cautiously.

"What's up? Ain't you from the Coast, cuz?" the young gorilla-looking goon asked. His French braids were surrounded by matted, nappy hair that looked like new growth. His skin was as black as coal. And he was ashy white on every bone that poked out.

"Yeah dat. This West Coast Rollin' 30's Crip, cuz. Where you from, bruh?" Shug balled his fists. The young gangsta looked vaguely familiar, but Shug couldn't quite place where he knew him from.

"I'm from West Coast too, cuz. I'm Big Chin-Check's lil brother. They call me Gangsta Blacc."

"Yeah, yeah, I remember you. You knocked out Money Mark from the Eastside in front of Fam Mart last year, huh?"

"Yup. Slept his bitch ass with the left, cuz!"

"How long you been up in here?" Shug inquired.

"Just a day. I'm about to get released in a few hours. All I had was a public intoxication charge. They makin' me dry out in here."

"Is that right? Check this out, lil homie. Let me holla atchu' real quick. I need you to do me a favor, cuz."

"Fo' sho', big homie. Just speak on it, and I got you, loc'."

Shug pulled the youngster aside and they whispered about thug bizness.

CHAPTER TWENTY-SEVEN
Where You Hide Your Cheese?

Wahdatah

As soon as I opened the front door, the cold morning air punched me in the face and pissed me off. My cell phone started ringing as I walked toward the Charger. *I gotta upgrade my whip game,* I thought. *Maybe flip me a big body Benz or a Navigator.*

"What's up, Tocarra?"

"Good morning, boo." Her voice made me smile.

"Good morning to you," I responded, dimples deep.

"Whatchu' got planned for the day?" she asked.

"Nothin' really. I was finna go pick some things up for the fridge. And then I gotta go see about making funeral arrangements for Drape. Why? What's up?"

"Nothing, I just wanted to let you know that they moved the book signing up to tomorrow. So I gotta adjust my schedule so I can make that happen."

"When do you think you'll be back?" I wasn't mad or upset, but I wasn't feeling the fact that I wouldn't be getting any pussy for the next couple days. Fucking up in Tocarra was becoming beautifully habitual.

"I should be back in town on Friday, hopefully. They want some of us to stay the weekend, but I'd rather spend mine with you."

"Like that?" I asked, flirting with her.

DEEPLY ROOTED

"You know it," she responded flirtatiously.

"And why is that?"

"Because you know how to make me feel good."

I heard footsteps behind me and inconspicuously reached for the fo'-five.

"Makin' you feel good makes me feel good, baby." I pulled the chrome out and turned with the quickness, ready to blast.

"Who the fuck is you, bruh!" I demanded to know. The fo'-five was about two-feet away from the gruff looking, black-as-a-boot thug's face.

"Chill, chill, chill, bruh." He held his hands up like I was robbing him. "I'm lookin' for Wahdatah. My name is Gangsta Blacc, and I got a message for him—for you. You kinda look like the big homie, Shug, so I'm assuming you're Wahdatah?" The dude looked hella grimy. He smelled even worse. My eyes narrowed and I cocked my head to the side when he mentioned my brother's name, and then a foul odor hit my nostrils hard.

"Damn, homie, is that you smellin' like that?" I backed up off his funky ass a couple steps. "Yeah, I'm Wah. What's up?" I told him, the pistol still winking at him.

"Yeah, that's me stankin' shit up. My bad, bruh. I just got out the county jail this morning, and I been sittin' up in that foul ass holding tank for damn near two days. Like I said, I just got released and the big homie Shug wanted me to personally deliver an important message to you. So I came straight here before going home. They got him on a double murder beef. They tryin' to say he killed the homie, Camron, and your boy Drape."

What the fuck? My mind was swimming in confusion.

"Talk to me. What's the message?" I asked him, but I was asking myself other questions. *Why the hell hadn't Miko contacted me? Why hadn't Shug hit me up on a three-way call? Why the fuck did the police arrest Shug for murders that I knew he didn't commit?*

"He said to tell you that he got set up by somebody, and the way it's lookin', he don't think that he gon' be able to make bail on no double homicide charges. He also told me to tell you to come see him the first chance you get. And if you can't come, then send your girl Tocarra. It's urgent business."

"Ai'ight, fo' sho'. How's my brother doin' up in there?"

"He straight. It's a few homies waitin' on him to go upstairs to general population, and one of the homies sent him a cool care package just before I bounced. Shug name ring bells on the streets, so it's all love up in there, you feel me?"

I asked a few more questions and got a few more answers. I wasn't finna hug on his stankin' ass. He was that funky, so I dapped his hand and hit him with fifty bucks so he could catch a cab and get himself something to eat.

In the course of me hearing Gangsta Blacc's footsteps, pulling out the banger, and drawing down on his ass, the call with Tocarra dropped. I called her back.

"Baby, sorry 'bout that. A situation came up on me." I explained in full detail everything that had happened, leaving nothing out.

"Shug said send me if you can't come? But why me, Wah? Why not Miko? Don't get me wrong, I don't have a problem with it; I'm just a little confused about why he wanna see me and not Miko?"

DEEPLY ROOTED

"Good question, baby, but I ain't got no answers for you,
ma. I'ma go see him on Saturday morning. If you ain't back
by then, I'll roll by myself. If you are back from your book
signing, then we can go together. That way you'll be
familiar with the process in the event you ever have to run
that trip again, ai'ight?"

"Okay, I'm cool with that."

Tocarra and I chopped it up for another half hour or so
before we ended our call.

I put off the food run and was back inside the crib
flipping through the Yellow Pages looking for a private
investigator. *He gone need a good lawyer too,* I thought as I
continued my search for legal assistance.

Knock. Knock. Knock.

Who the fuck is this? I reached behind me and gripped
the chrome, keeping the fo'-five hidden.

"Who is it?" came out my mouth.

"It's me, Miko."

'Bout fuckin' time! I thought, tucking the chrome at the
small of my back. I twisted the doorknob and pulled the
door open.

"What's good, Miko?" I hugged her and invited her
inside. She stepped in and took her coat off.

"Have a seat. Make yourself comfortable," I told her and
made my way over to the wet bar. "What you drinkin' on,
sis?" I asked her, not letting her know how suspicious I felt.

"Do you have a Vitamin Water?"

"Yup, actually I do. Here." I walked it over to her.

ICE MIKE

I took a seat and sipped on some orange juice, and then fired up a stick of Green Gorilla Kush. Shit was strong as fuck. Like the Incredible Hulk.

We talked for a minute, when a thought socked me in the head. *How the fuck did Miko know where I lived?* I didn't know if it was the trees activating my antennae or what, but ever since I discovered that Shug was my brother, Miko had never been to my crib. I distinctly remembered that fact because I had commented on it the other day when I was at his crib. I had invited him over to come kick it with me and Tocarra in the near future and bring her along.

I looked across the room, and we made eye contact. She had this look on her face that could best be described as angry, twisted with sly. It unnerved me.

She peered at me over the bottle of water. "So, tell me, Wah? Where the hell did you hide all your cheese? I mean, Shug is scared to put his money in the bank. So I'm just wondering if you share the same fear?"

No this bitch didn't just ask me about my money! I looked at her like she was crazy. That shit knocked me all the way off balance. *She been in my spot for five minutes and ain't mentioned nothing about my brother getting gaffled up for the murders of our two closest homies, but here she is asking about my paper.* The hair on the back of my neck stood up. I walked back over to the bar thinking on some hella foul shit.

"Miko, where the fuck is Shug at?" I pulled the fo'-five out from the back of my waistband and tucked it in the front once I was behind the wet bar. While I was sitting on the couch, it occurred to me that the gun was behind me, much more difficult to reach like that.

"Uh, he called me and told me that uh . . . that you already knew he was locked up," she stammered. Her words came with uncertainty behind them. I could tell she was making that shit up as she went along, as if she wasn't prepared for my sudden line of questioning.

I walked back to the sofa. I didn't want to be rude and boot her ass out, but I didn't trust her one bit. Even though she was my brother's fiancée, my gut was warning me about her. *Something about this bitch ain't right!*

Ring. Ring. Ring.

My cell phone started ringing.

That's when I fucked up and made the most critical mistake of my life. I stood up to dig the phone out of my pocket. "Hello?"

Bang!

A searing heat ripped into my stomach and burned like nothing I had ever felt in my life. I dropped the phone and clutched at my gut, instinctively reacting to the flash of pain that felt like a fire had been lit inside of me. *This bitch shot me!* It dawned on me as my mind tried to do the math.

Bang!

A second shot tore into my T-shirt, and again that incredibly hot pain burned somewhere deep inside the pit of my stomach. My mind kicked into survival-mode. I jumped back onto the couch, trying to put some distance between me and that dirty bitch. Another bullet hit me in the chest as I reached for my chrome. My eyes widened with fear. I was already beginning to feel the effects from being lit up three times. The burning sensation in my body felt like hot lava being poured inside the holes in my stomach. As I fell backward, for some strange reason I remembered thinking, *That's a .380 in that bitch hand.*

From that moment on, everything seemed to be going in super slow motion. The pain in my chest burned like a wildfire. I felt the fo'-five drop from my hand. The living room window gave way under the pressure of my body forcefully falling against it. I heard the loud crash of glass, and then I felt shards of glass raining down on me.

Bang!

Another gunshot exploded. I felt another burst of white hot pain stab me in the shoulder, and then my head hit the concrete outside, hard with a sickening thud. A slide show of thoughts began playing across the back of my eyelids— memories from my childhood. My granny smiling at me with love in her eyes, Tocarra kissing my lips, sitting up under the lemon tree, finding out who my brother was and meeting him at IHOP.

Bang!

Another bullet hit me.

I'm shot the fuck up. Is this my life flashing before my eyes? Am I dying?

Then my world went dark. Pitch black, and I felt nothing.

DEEPLY ROOTED

CHAPTER TWENTY-EIGHT
Hidden Treasure

Miko

I know that son of a bitch ain't hid that money nowhere outside of this ma'fuckin' house!" Miko said to herself after plugging Wahdatah with four shots. The excitement that coursed throughout her body went beyond the pleasure of an orgasm. What she had finally been able to accomplish was amongst the sweetest of joys.

Before going off to search for the hidden treasure, she stepped up onto the sofa and looked down on Wahdatah's twisted frame lying motionless on the ground.

Bang! Bang!

Two more slugs hit his body and buried deep inside of him. She stuffed the .380 in her back pocket and went about tearing up his house in search of his half of the money that had once been buried under the lemon tree. *Where the fuck could that money be?*

The bedroom!

It seemed to be the most likely of places to start looking. It made the most sense, and she was seriously pressed for time. The po-po would definitely be on their way after all that shooting in this upscale neighborhood.

Bingo!

A couple of minutes into her search, she discovered the hidden treasure in the back of his closet. On her way out, the briefcase sitting on top of the bed caught her eye. She walked over to it and opened it up. Her heart orgasmed when she saw the jewelry and the stacks of rubber band wrapped big faces inside of it.

It only took her a couple of minutes to load all of the stuff into her car. She had to hurry; the sound of fast approaching sirens could be heard in the distance. They were getting louder, closer.

The bottle of water!

Panic punched her in the gut. That water bottle had her DNA on it. She had to go back in there and get it! Miko ran as fast as she could and snatched up the half-empty bottle of Vitamin Water before making a mad dash to the safety of her car. Her whip was nearing the end of the block when the first of four cop cars came flying past her, headed in the opposite direction. She stole a peek out of her window as she turned left and saw them come to a screeching halt in front of Wahdatah's house.

* * * * *

Tocarra

Tocarra pushed a button on her phone and a smile spread across her face when Wahdatah had answered with a simple "Hello?" Her heart skipped a beat. Then she heard what sounded like a gunshot, and her heart dropped to the pit of her stomach.

"Wah? Is that you? Are you okay? Wahdatah!" she screamed into the phone.

Another gunshot.

Her body jumped at the sickening sound. Tears spilled over her eyelids and rolled down her face. Her heart beat increased to a dangerous point.

Then another gunshot. And another.

"Wahdatah! Baby, please say something to me!" she pleaded into the phone that shook in her hand.

Bang! Bang!

Two more gunshots.

The most horrible sounds she had ever heard.

"Noooooooooo!" Tocarra screamed her heart-wrenching anguish into the phone.

She ended the call and pressed 911 on her phone. After several failed attempts to tell the operator what had just occurred, she was finally able to give an accurate account of what she had heard. She provided the operator with Wahdatah's address and ended the call.

Tocarra jumped into the fire engine red 750 Li BMW Wahdatah had recently bought for her and smashed her foot down on the gas in the direction of his house. The 24-inch chrome Hypnotic wheels were eating up the distance between her house and his.

When she arrived, he was already in the back of an ambulance. She ran up to it as they were closing the door. She could hear some of the EMTs conversation in the back of the ambulance.

"He's lost a tremendous amount of blood. We're gonna have to hurry. I don't think he's gonna make it!" one of the EMT's screamed out.

"His vitals are dropping. Give me some—"

"Excuse me, miss, but this is a crime scene. I'm going to have to ask you to step behind the yellow tape here." A police officer interrupted her ear hustle and pointed to the sidewalk across the street.

"My name is Tocarra Rhodes-Robinson. That's my boyfriend in there!" she informed the cop.

"I understand, ma'am. But—"

"What hospital are they taking him to?" she yelled to the EMT, ignoring the cop in front of her.

"Paradise Valley Hospital, ma'am."

"Thank you."

Tocarra was in the BMW trying her damnedest to get to the hospital before the ambulance got there.

* * * * *

Wahdatah

I could hear what was going on around me. The chaos that surrounded me sounded like Charlie Brown's teacher. *Whomp-whomp-whomp-wah-whomp-whomp-whomp-wah.*

Then I heard a loud voice in my ear. "He's lost a tremendous amount of blood!"

Then the voice of an angel.

"I'm Tocarra Rhodes-Robinson. That's my boyfriend in there!"

I blacked out for a minute.

When I came to, the pain inside my stomach was unbearable. It felt like my blood was on fire. I thought about the last time Tocarra and I kissed; then I blacked out again.

* * * * *

Miko

"No, Miko. Something ain't right! I don't give a damn about what the police are tryin' to say. I know damn well Shug ain't killed Camron," Monisha said.

"It doesn't matter what we think, or what we know, Mo. We gotta look at this from a realistic standpoint. Shug is in jail for two murders, and they say they have evidence against him that ties him to each murder."

"So what! Girl, you know like I know that people get set-up all the time."

"We'll talk about it later. Right now I need to take a shower."

Miko's attitude about the entire ordeal was rubbing Monisha the wrong way. After Miko went to take her shower, Monisha went to the kitchen to fix herself a drink. She desperately needed to numb her pain. On her way back to the couch, she noticed the briefcase.

"That looks like Wah's briefcase," she murmured.

After finishing her drink, she poured herself another one. Monisha sat down and nursed the drink on the couch, but her eyes kept returning to the briefcase. The pull of suspicious curiosity was irresistible. It was as if she was drawn to it, drawn to the luggage Miko brought in with her.

Feeling the effects of the two drinks, and with curiosity provoking her need to know, she went over to do a closer inspection on the suitcase.

"Oh my goodness!" Monisha opened the briefcase and almost screamed. Fainting was a breath away. She slapped her hand over her mouth and stepped back. The sight of stacks and stacks of big faces had a staggering effect on her. She picked up her phone and hurriedly dialed a number.

Answer your phone, Wahdatah! Pick up! Pick up! Pick up, damn it! she screamed in her head, waiting for an answer.

The voice behind her scared the shit out of her.

"You shouldn't be snooping around in my stuff, Mo. Your nosy ass shoulda left well enough alone." Miko's voice was frosty.

A shiver of fear ran down Monisha's spinal column. "What the fuck have you done, Miko?" Monisha's questioned was laced with anger.

Bang! Bang! Bang!

Was Miko's only explanation.

The three bullets killed Monisha instantly. Her body, a twisted mess sprawled out awkwardly on the living room floor.

ICE MIKE

CHAPTER TWENTY-NINE
Hella Slippin'

Shug

Shug waited in the long line of inmates with an angry scowl on his dissatisfied face. The punk ass judge had just ordered that he stay in jail, hitting him with a three million dollar bail. Producing three million wasn't the problem; the problem was that the government would confiscate every damn dollar if somebody showed up at the bail bondsman's door with that type of loot.

Fuck it, thought Shug as the deputy wrapped waist chains around his midsection. The handcuffs and leg shackles fit tightly around his wrist and ankles. His chains were attached to the fat Mexican cat with the shaved, tattooed head in front of him, and the tall, dark skinned brotha behind him.

The long, slow trek back to the county jail was filled with all kinds of thoughts that had been running around in his mind for the past few days. *Who the fuck really killed Camron and Drape? Why the fuck Miko ain't been down here to see me yet? Where the hell is my brother? Did Gangsta Blacc deliver that message for me? What the fuck type of evidence do these dirty ass crackers got that implicate me? Which one of the ma'fuckas next to me is smellin' like a bag of hot wet shit?* He couldn't wait to get back to his cell block, so he could kick back and produce some answers to some of the questions that bombarded his brain.

"What's up, cuz?" one of his homeboys asked, before firing up a stick of kush.

"What up, big homie? At least now I know why I couldn't find you when I was ready to put you on."

"Homie, I been in here for months now. This shit ain't new to me. How did it go in court today?"

"It was hella ugly in that ma'fucka, homie, but I expected that. So it wasn't no surprise, you feel me? What I wasn't expectin' was to feel so ma'fuckin' twisted when them bitch ass white folks announced the charges and said the homie Camron's name. That fucked me up hearing his name on the other end of my murder charge." Shug accepted the thin joint his homie handed him and pulled on it hard.

"Even though me and Cam didn't get along over that Monisha shit, all the homies feel some kind of way about the way he got murked. But er'body know how tight you and the homie Cam was, so ain't none of the homies questioning whether or not you killed him. What the fuck can't nobody figure out though is who got something to gain by pinning that shit on you?" Boscoe was one of Shug's old school homeboys, a real banger who had put in major work back in the day, and who was one of the more respected homies from his set.

"I don't even know, bruh. But like the saying goes: Everything in the dark eventually gon' come to the light." He pulled on the joint again and held the potent smoke in until his chest couldn't hold his breath any longer.

"You fuck with that crystal meth, Shug?" Boscoe asked out of curiosity, offering Shug a knot of white powder.

ICE MIKE

"Naw, Boscoe. I don't fuck with nothin' but trees and drank."

"Ai'ight, I'm just checkin'. If you need anything else, bruh, holla at me and I'll see what I can do about it." Boscoe had plenty of connections. He was a crafty veteran of the prison system who had a way with words, so he made things happen when and where the average person couldn't.

"Now that you mention it, bruh. How can I get my hands on a cell phone, cuz? I need to make a few phone calls."

"Say no more, homie. I gotchu'. I'll be back in a minute." Boscoe left and returned several minutes later with a Samsung smart phone. "Shit, all you had to do was ask, cuz. We got three of these ma'fuckas floatin' around on the block."

"Good lookin' out, Boscoe. I hella need this."

Shug's entire mood shifted from somber to hyped-up once he held the cell phone in his hand. He sat down on the bottom bunk and contemplated his next move.

Ring. Ring. Ring.

He blew his brother's cell phone up, but every time he called it went to voicemail. He finally decided to leave a message. Not knowing Wah's circumstances, he chose his words carefully and revealed little when he left the message. Shug wanted to call Miko, but his gut was telling him to let her show her true colors while he was in this predicament. Something about her actions had him on 'noid. *Why do I feel like my future wifey is on some foul shit?*

Instead he tried to holla at Camron's girl. His heart went out to Monisha, knowing that she had to be seriously suffering, trying to cope with the loss of Camron's brutal murder.

DEEPLY ROOTED

Ring. Ring. Ring.

Shug waited for Monisha to pick up.

"Hello?"

"Hey, what's up?" Shug's eyes squinted tight with bewilderment.

"Who is this?" the soft, sexy voice was all too familiar.

Shug pulled the phone away from his ear and looked at it strangely, like it was a Martian's upside down pussy. His mind raced to recover from his surprise. He quickly thought of something and put his shirt over his mouth in an attempt to distort his voice.

"Uh yeah, this Tommy. Is Monisha available?" He put baritone on his verbals, and squared his delivery trying to sound like someone else.

"Naw, she ain't available right now. Call back on Monday 'cause she out of town for the weekend." Shug recognized his fiancée's voice the minute he heard it.

"Ai'ight then. Tell her Tommy called."

"Okay, I sure will."

Why the fuck was Miko answering Monisha's phone? If Monisha was out of town, she woulda took her phone with her! What the hell was she up to? Shug was stuck on stupid. He held the phone in his hand, wearing a look of stunned disbelief. *Wow! Now I know for a fact that something is going on with my girl.*

He couldn't remember any other numbers off the top of his head, so he gave the phone back to Boscoe while thinking, *Shug, you hella slippin'.*

CHAPTER THIRTY
Watch Out

Tocarra

The ambulance came to a screeching halt at the hospital emergency room entrance. A rolling gurney being guided by a team of nurses and EMTs pushed past the open sliding doors. Vital signs were being announced in a loud, clear voice. Instructions were issued out in a firm, commanding manner. A descriptive account of the exact location of every gunshot wound was being rattled off like an itemized list. An oxygen mask covered Wahdatah's mouth and nose.

"He's flat-lining!" one of the nurses screamed out.

More instructions were issued. More vital sign announcements. It wasn't looking good for Wahdatah.

Minutes after the ambulance arrived, Tocarra's red BMW jerked to a stop, and she jumped out as soon as she shut the luxury whip down. She ran as fast as the Jimmy Choo pumps would allow her to, until she was at the front desk.

"Wahdatah Mitchell! I'm looking for a Wahdatah Mitchell, who was just brought in after being shot."

After receiving directions, Tocarra was off and running. They stopped her at the doors leading to surgery.

"You can't go back there, ma'am," a nurse wearing a smock with blood smeared all over it said to her.

244

"Is he gonna make it? Please tell me that he's gonna make it!" Tocarra started crying hard into the palms of her cupped hands.

"It's touch and go right now, ma'am, but I can assure you that we have a very capable staff back there working on him. Please, follow me so we can get some information from you, okay?" The nurse's voice was soft and soothing; her demeanor was calm and settling.

Tocarra knew there was little else she could do other than pray, hope, and wait, and that's exactly what she spent the next few hours doing.

After realizing she would be at the hospital for an extended period, she called her publisher to be excused from the book signing, citing a family emergency as her reason. Tocarra then filled out the necessary paperwork while sitting in the crowded waiting room.

"Tocarra Rhodes-Robinson?" Another nurse wearing a blood-stained outfit called her name hours later.

"Yes, I am she." Tocarra held her breath while waiting for the nurse to speak on Wahdatah's condition.

"I-I need you to follow me."

"Is he okay? Is he gonna make it?" she asked the nurse, desperation hanging off her every word.

Once they were out of earshot of the room full of onlookers, the nurse introduced Tocarra to the doctor who had performed the surgery.

"I'm Doctor Gerald Hayes, Mr. Mitchell's surgeon."

"How is he?" she blurted out before the doctor could go on. Her hands twisted the bundle of tissues that one of the hospital workers had given her.

"The surgery was successful, Ms. Rhodes-Robinson—successful in the sense that we were able to extract all of the bullets and stop the internal bleeding."

"Thank you Jesus!" Tocarra praised her Lord and Savior.

"However, Mr. Mitchell's condition remains very grave. He's far from out of harm's way. I'm sorry to have to tell you this, but Mr. Mitchell is currently in a comatose state, and to be quite honest with you, when it comes to matters such as these, there's just simply no telling when he will recover, or if he will even awaken from the coma."

"A coma? What the hell do you mean he's in a coma?"

Doctor Hayes further explained the surgical procedure Wahdatah had undergone, his condition, and all of the possibilities that came with it. He tried to prepare Tocarra for what it would be like, painting a picture of past comatose patients and the loved-ones involved, the broken expectations, as well as all of the heart-wrenching survival stories.

"Can I go see him?"

"Yes, but prepare yourself for the harsh reality that he will not be able to respond to you in anyway whatsoever. Nurse, please assist Ms. Rhodes-Robinson." The doctor turned and walked off, leaving the two women standing there.

When Tocarra went in to see Wahdatah, she entered the room on unsteady legs. Her heart broke at the sight of him hooked up to all of the machines and monitors. His face was swollen to nearly twice its normal size. A huge tube was taped to his mouth, and a bag inflated then deflated with every breath he took. She stood with both hands covering her mouth. Tears streamed down her face in a steady flow. A fearful whimper escaped her lips.

The nurse touched her on the shoulder. "Will you be okay?" she asked her.

Tocarra nodded slowly in silence.

"Put it in prayer. Let go and let God," the nurse whispered to her, and then left her and Wahdatah alone.

Tocarra stood completely still in the same position for several moments. Tears blurred her vision. Finally, she walked to his bedside and paused. The non-stop beeping of his life, the one thing Tocarra was thankful for. The sounds of the other machines and monitors, a tormenting symphony to her spirit.

"Oh, baby!" She cried harder at the sight of his bullet-riddled body. Every fiber of her being went out to him. "Who did this to you, Wah?" Tocarra hugged herself and wept softly. She leaned over and kissed him tenderly on the side of his face. "Please don't leave me, Wahdatah," she whispered against his ear. "You are a strong, beautiful black king, and you have so much more to offer the world. You can't leave me now, baby. The world needs you."

* * * * *

Wahdatah

"Oh baby, who did this to you, Wah?" I heard Tocarra's angelic voice in my ear.

Miko. That dirty bitch Miko is the one who did this to me! I screamed out loud in my mind.

"Please don't leave me, Wahdatah. You are a strong, beautiful black king, and you have so much more to offer the world. You can't leave me now, baby. The world needs you." Her words were like a soft song in my ear.

I ain't going nowhere, ma. I still got a gang of livin' to do, baby, I yelled as loud as I could in my brain. I tried to move my lips and make my mouth work, but it wasn't happening.

It finally dawned on me that no matter how hard I tried, no matter how loud I yelled in my head, she couldn't hear me. I wasn't able to speak. *Keep trying!* I planned on coming out of this coma one day. And when that day came, I wanted to still have the ability of speech. My mind was fully functioning. I was going to exercise speaking as much as I could, until I could finally talk again. I wanted to hold Tocarra in my arms again. I wanted to laugh and chill with my brother again. We hadn't had enough time to truly bond and get to know each other in a real way like brothers are supposed to.

More than anything else though, I wanted to kill. I wanted to look that bitch Miko in her eyes and see her shake in her stilettos when she realizes that it is by my hand that she takes her last breath.

* * * * *

Tocarra

Tocarra was by Wahdatah's bedside for as long as they would allow her. For nearly two days straight she was attached to his hip. She caressed his face with her fingers and spoke to him, often whispering in his ear. She sat next to him holding his hand, talking aloud about any and every thought that crossed her mind. Her heart broke again when she overheard one of the nurses mention that she was the only known family member that Wahdatah had.

Then the thought of his brother Shug roared a reminder to her. Wahdatah was supposed to go visit Shug in jail! Shug didn't even know that Wahdatah had been shot!

She leaned closer against his ear. "Baby, I almost forgot that we were supposed to go visit your brother today! He probably doesn't even know that you've been shot, Wah! You said that Shug stressed to you that if you weren't able to go see him, then he wanted me to visit him." She kissed his lips softly. "I'm gonna go home and take a shower and change my clothes. Then I'ma go try to see Shug down at the county jail, okay?" She continued to speak to him, and then prayed with him for a while.

An hour or so later, she took his hands in hers and whispered her love for him in his ear before she left.

* * * * *

Wahdatah

I knew that I could count on you, baby. I didn't doubt for a second that you were a thorough ass chick, Tocarra. Go 'head and see my brother. Handle that and let him know what's up with me.

I was yelling inside my head, hoping she could hear me. *I love you too, baby.* I wanted to warn her about Miko.

Tocarra, be careful, baby! Watch out for that bitch, Miko. Did you hear me? Tocarra? Tocarra!

CHAPTER THIRTY-ONE
A Startling Revelation

Shug

"M arcellus Braxton, you have a visit!" the guard barked out loud.

It's about time. Shug put the book down that had had his attention hostage. *White Lines* by Tracy Brown had intrigued the thug, who felt like the classic urban novel paralleled his own life story in many ways.

One of the best urban books I ever read, Shug mused as he washed up and made himself presentable. He donned a crisp new jail issued jumpsuit and the fresh pair of kicks he had been allowed to retrieve when he was arrested. Then he sat back down on his bunk and waited for the law to come get him for his visit.

Nearly fifteen minutes passed before Shug walked into the visiting area. Automatically, his eyes scanned the sea of black and brown faces for his brother. His eyebrows rose up when he caught sight of Tocarra, her beauty putting to shame all the other chicks in the room.

He wore a smile that clearly expressed his happiness at seeing a familiar face. There was swag with every step he took. It naturally oozed off him like cologne; people just sensed it. Females sitting with their boyfriends dared to stare longer than they should have. Inmates twisted their necks around after he walked by, some, out of curiosity, others out of anger.

DEEPLY ROOTED

They both picked the phone up at the same time.

"What's up, girl? It's good to see you. You look nice by the way. Where's Wah?" he asked, respectfully complimenting his brother's girl. The worried look on Tocarra's face warned him of bad news. "What's wrong, Tocarra? Sit down. Are you all right?" Shug looked around the room, glad that no po-po were around.

"It's Wah, Shug," she said full of sadness.

"What about Wah?" Shug asked, concern was written all over his face.

"He's in the hospital. Somebody shot him up bad." Her voice cracked when she spoke and she broke down into tears and dabbed a tissue carefully under her eyes.

"What? Nah . . . aw hell nah!" Tears threatened to fall over his eyelids as he fought to maintain his composure. "Do they know who did it? Is he gonna make it?" The thought of losing the brother he had recently grown so close to was too much for even the street hardened thug. A stream of tears slowly rolled down his face and dotted his jumpsuit.

"Bitch, you was jockin' this soft ass nigga?" the inmate seated next to Shug asked the question sarcastically to his girlfriend, who was on the other side of the glass. He jerked his thumb in Shug's direction. "He over there cryin' like a broad and you was sweatin' that fool!" His words dripped with disgust.

"Fuck you say, nigga!" Shug pushed himself up with one arm and threw a violent three-piece that savagely connected to the inmate's chin, temple, and mouth. The tough talking inmate's forehead smacked the metal tabletop in front of him, and his body locked up and went into a fist-forced slumber.

ICE MIKE

The inmate's girlfriend knocked on the glass and called his name through the phone. Dude wasn't budging.

"Bitch ass nigga, get up!" she made one final attempt to wake her knocked out man up before leaving the room in a huff, embarrassed that her dude had been knocked the fuck out.

Tocarra watched the violent spectacle with wide-eyed shock from her ringside seat, amazed.

"Sorry you had to see that, Tocarra, but that bitch ass ma'fucka needed that." Shug wiped himself down and took his seat and put the phone to his ear.

"I understand. He had that comin'. Anyway though, the doctors say that it's too soon to tell what Wah's recovery will be like. They don't even know if he'll come out of the coma. And no, the police don't have a clue about who shot him."

Shug shook his head sadly and fought back tears. "Damn, that's fucked up. Are you okay?"

"No, but I feel a little better when I'm by his side. He needs me there." Her eyes filled with tears too.

Shug stared into her eyes intently. "I'm glad that it's you who's by his side. It's comforting knowing that he has a solid woman in his corner. Real talk, Tocarra. If I can't be there by his side then I can't think of a better person than you to be there with him."

They chopped it up for a while before Shug got at her about an issue that needed attention. She looked into his eyes trying to read what his need of her was. "What's up, Shug? What do you need?"

He told her of his suspicions and asked her to do something that may have been out of her league. She told him to commit her cell phone number to memory and call her tomorrow and his problem would be fixed. She would do her best to see to it.

* * * * *

Tocarra

Doubt began to fill her mind as she made her exit from the prison. *You can do this*, Tocarra told herself. *Just stick to the plan.* On her way through the crowded parking lot en route to her car, Tocarra looked up and happened to notice the prominent red-brick library with the lush green grass surrounded by six-foot high wrought iron black gates. The landscape was meticulously manicured, bushes and trees trimmed and tapered to perfection. She thought about how she went to the library to do research before writing a book. A thought crossed her mind and then settled into her determination before finally provoking her into action. Tocarra pulled one of the huge double-doors open and walked inside.

Originally, her intentions were to go inside the library and research the history of Marquis 'Bad Boy' Mitchell. She thought it would be a good idea to find out as much as she could about Wahdatah and Shug's father, so she could then relate whatever information she discovered to Wahdatah during her long talks at his bedside. Her heart wanted badly to believe that sitting by his side and talking to him about his father would be a way of planting seeds into his subconscious that would hopefully sprout and bloom into memories once he awakened from his comatose state. In doing so, she stumbled across a startling revelation that blew her mind, something she never would have guessed.

ICE MIKE

*No, it couldn't be! I don't think that Wah or Shug knows anything about any of this—*Her eyes widened with shock—her breath became stuck in her throat. Tocarra's hand moved frantically as she hurriedly scribbled down notes. Her heart beat wildly with incredulous disbelief. Tocarra couldn't believe what she was reading . . .

Reputed drug kingpin Kiko Dunbar was brutally gunned down early yesterday morning in what police are now calling a drug related homicide. Dunbar was shot eleven times by an 18-year-old African American male, who police have now identified as Marquis Mitchell. Mitchell was subsequently apprehended by sheriff deputies as he attempted to flee the scene of the crime.

Kiko Dunbar was rumored to be one of the most feared and prosperous drug traffickers in California. Kiko Dunbar is survived by a five-year-old daughter, Miko Dunbar.

Tocarra printed out a copy of the newspaper article and folded it in half before stuffing it into her clutch.

"Hurry the hell up and call me, Shug, so I can drop this bomb on you!" she muttered as she sprinted to the 750 Li. She punched the ignition with her thumb and whipped the fire-engine red BMW into traffic. After leaving the library Tocarra was even more dead set on carrying out the promise she had made earlier to Shug at their visit.

"Pick up! Pick up! Pick up, Miko!" Tocarra said desperately as she maneuvered the luxury ride with one hand while holding the cell phone against her ear with the other.

"Hello?" Miko's voice was tentative with suspicion.

"Hey, Miko. What's up, girl? Are you okay?" Tocarra's voice was laced with concern.

DEEPLY ROOTED

"No, not really. They won't let me in to see my baby, Shug, and I just found out that somebody killed my best friend Monisha. I'm very shook up right now to be perfectly honest with you. What about you? How's it going? I haven't heard from Wah these past coupla days. Is he straight?" Miko was as crafty as she was cold-blooded. She wasn't about to expose her hand to anybody, not this late in the game.

"Wah is in the hospital, Miko. He was shot six times a couple of days ago, and now he's in a coma." Tocarra's voice cracked with emotion.

"What! Are you serious? Oh my goodness, girl! I am so sorry to hear that. Is there anything I can do to help?" Miko was not only crafty and cold-blooded, but she was devious as well.

"Actually, yes, there is something you can do. I need somebody to talk to about everything that is going on. I swear I feel like I'm about to lose my mind!" Tocarra was amazed at how smoothly things were going. Miko was falling right into Shug's plan, walking right into their trap.

"No, I don't mind at all, girl. When and where do you want to meet?" Miko wore a sinister smile on her face on the other end of the phone. *This game-goofy bitch is makin' this shit so easy! Killing her ass is going to be a piece of cake.*

"How about that little seafood cafe down at Seaport Village? You know the one we went to about a month ago."

"Okay, when?" Miko asked with a scandalous smile.

"Tomorrow. Noonish?"

"All right, girl. See you tomorrow around twelve then." Miko disconnected the call and pulled the .380 out of her purse. She pulled the clip out and inspected it before shoving it back into the handle. *Bitch, I'ma give it to you just like I gave it to your man, only this time I'ma finish yo' ass off.*

Tocarra stuffed her phone into her purse and went about following Shug's plan to a tee.

DEEPLY ROOTED

CHAPTER THIRTY-TWO
Up to No Good

Tocarra

Tocarra kissed Wahdatah's cheek and whispered, "I love you" against his lips before she took off to meet with Miko.

Twenty minutes later, she was at the ocean front cafe. She noticed Miko already sitting outside under an umbrella at one of the tables on the sidewalk.

Miko smiled a fake smile when she saw Tocarra approaching. "Hey girl! What's up wit' it? How are you doing?" Tocarra greeted Miko joyfully and pulled her hand out of her pocket just like she had practiced doing at least fifty times over the past twenty-four hours.

"I'm good. How about you?" Miko answered, looking around before relaxing her grip on the .380 as Tocarra neared her. *Not now,* she thought, *too many witnesses.*

The two beautiful women embraced. Tocarra was able to inconspicuously tag Miko with one of the pea-sized miniature recording devices just like Shug had instructed her. They sat down and talked for a while over lunch, chicken salads.

Fifteen minutes into the mid-day meal, when it appeared to be as good a time as any to kill her, Miko slyly reached her hand under the table, and ever so slowly slid it into her purse. Her fingers snaked around the small pistol's frame, and her index finger eagerly caressed the surface of the trigger. She smiled over her drink and pulled the .380 out. It was pointed at Tocarra's stomach under the table.

Die bitch! Miko began to squeeze. But then she was forced to put the murder on pause when a couple walked out of the cafe and strolled hand in hand right past their table.

"Excuse me for a second, Miko." Tocarra rose suddenly and pulled her phone out. She stepped away from the table and turned to talk into the phone. Something about Miko's body language warned Tocarra that she was up to no good. Shug had warned her to be extra cautious and to stay on her tiptoes at all times.

Unbeknownst to her, the move saved her life. Several more couples stumbled out of the cafe laughing loudly. Tocarra used the crowd as a witness and a way out.

"That was an important call, Miko. I'm sorry, but I have to rush off now. It's an emergency. Let's hook up again another time, okay?" She pecked Miko's cheek with a fake kiss and turned to leave, walking away and blending in with the raucous crowd.

"Okay, sure thing," Miko said to her back. "You lucky bitch!" she whispered angrily into her glass as she downed the rest of her drink.

She put the gun back inside her purse and zipped it closed. She slung the purse over her shoulder and jumped into her car, vowing to kill Tocarra the next chance she got.

* * * * *

Miko

Damn, I wish I would've shot that lucky ass bitch! She could be a liability. Miko rested her whip against the curb and opened the door. She put one foot on the asphalt outside the car and reached across the console and grabbed the beautiful floral arrangement she had picked up after having lunch with Tocarra. She was still fuming at missing her golden opportunity to pop that bitch and tie up another loose end. It was that very anger that persuaded her to come here today.

Hopefully, talking to her father would lift her spirits and help clear her mind, as it had so many other times when she was a young girl, after being released from the mental hospital.

She walked for several minutes before arriving at his gravesite. As she had always done in the past when she came to visit her father, she said a silent prayer and set the flowers against his headstone.

Miko sat with her back against the huge granite stone and got comfortable. For a few minutes, the five-year-old little girl revealed herself and cried silent tears of pain over the loss of her father. The tears flowed freely as she reminisced about the days when her daddy would take her all around the world, the fun she had when she was alone with him, and it was just the two of them on daddy/daughter day. How he spoiled her and gave her the world. Bouncing her on his knee, and Miko laughing hysterically.

The pain over the loss of her father at such a young age was catastrophically traumatic. The pain and hurt was deeply rooted and it never lessened. In fact, it only grew worse. At one time it had become too much, and it broke her mentally. She lost her love for humanity when she discovered her hatred for mankind.

Miko sat there with her back to the headstone and released her pain. Tears streamed down her face and her voice cracked with emotion.

DEEPLY ROOTED

She sounded like a young girl when she spoke. "Hi Daddy, how have you been? I know it's been a long time since I last stopped by to see you, but I made a promise to you the last time I was here that I wouldn't come back until I avenged your death and got even with the person responsible for puttin' you in this dirt."

"Well, I did it, Daddy! I kept my promise and I avenged your death properly. I even took it a step farther, Daddy, and got back every dime of the money that he stole from you. All of it and some more. You would be so proud of your baby girl, Daddy. I guess it just runs in the family, huh?" Miko giggled girlishly and got lost in her thoughts of yesteryear.

The young girl's voice was gone; talking now was a grown woman. "You know, the last time I was here I had just murdered both of his baby mamas' on my birthday. Boom! Boom! Point blank to the face on both of those bitches on the same day, on my day! My gift to me for him taking you away from me." A wicked smile and closed eyes received the experience.

After a minute of mentally revisiting one of her finest accomplishments Miko continued, "Anyway, let me tell you how your baby girl finished the game, Daddy."

Miko went on to describe how she intentionally hooked up with Shug several years after her cousins Cream and Suspect went to prison on manslaughter charges. How she decided to get with him in hopes of locating the five million dollars that had been stolen from her father twenty-three years ago. How her plan worked. How she convinced the silly trick, Jracia to kill Camron and Drape, so that she could then set Shug up for the double murders and send him away to prison forever because death would've been too easy of a penalty to pay. She wanted him to suffer emotionally forever. Then killing Jracia to cover her own tracks. She excitedly told him about shooting up Wahdatah, and then Monisha's nosy ass, and how she would take care of Tocarra once the opportunity presented itself.

"I got plans, Daddy. I got big plans to take over the streets and run the dope game just like you did it. Cream and Suspect are scheduled to be released in the next year, but I ain't waitin' on them because I got some hungry young thugs from the Eastside that I've been hollerin' at, who been starving in the game, and they are ready to tear some shit up for me. I got the money. I got the connection, and I got a small army of savages, Daddy. Now it's your little girl's time to shine in the game. I swear I ain't finna show the streets no love, Daddy. No love because they ain't never showed me none!" She went on for a while longer about her plans to become a Queen Pin, the coldest, most ruthless and successful Queen Pin that ever breathed in air.

DEEPLY ROOTED

CHAPTER THIRTY-THREE
Rotten Schemes

Tocarra

Tocarra sat next to Wahdatah's hospital bed and put the recorder up to the phone and pushed play. Miko's voice coldly retold the accounts of her past and present deeds. Killing both Wahdatah and Shug's mothers on her eighteenth birthday. A birthday gift to herself, were her exact words. Having Drape and Camron murdered, and then killing the girl who had unknowingly did her bidding. Setting up her fiancé, and sending him to jail for those same murders. Shooting Wahdatah in his house six times in her attempt to kill him too. And her plans to kill Tocarra the first opportunity she got. The plans she had of filling her father's big shoes, and using the money to make a name for herself in the dope game and becoming the biggest boss bitch. How she vowed to be the most ruthless Queen Pin to ever set up shop in San Diego. Miko was plotting rotten schemes in an effort to realize her dreams.

* * * * *

Shug

Shug sat in his jail cell with the cell phone pressed against his ear and the meanest mug he had ever worn as he listened to his fiancée talk about her sinister past. His mind was desperately trying to figure out a way of coming from

DEEPLY ROOTED

up under the two murder charges he was facing, murder charges that could send him away forever.

He couldn't turn the recording over to the police because he wasn't built like that. Besides, involving the police would mean exposing the millions of dollars, and risk possibly getting all of that shit confiscated.

No, he would have to find another way to get from behind these bars, so he could get at that dirty bitch, Miko, his former fiancée, the woman he once loved with all his heart. A woman he now hated with a passion that he could not put into words. His was a hatred he could only express with action, a violent, murderous kind of action.

* * * * *

Wahdatah

I vowed to fight with every fiber in my body to come up out of this coma. That bitch Miko had to die. She murdered my mother! She murked my man Drape! That punk ass bitch tried to kill me! *I don't give a fuck what it takes. I put that on everything I love that I will overcome this coma, and I will kill that bitch, Miko if it's the last thing I do on this earth!*

* * * * *

Tocarra

Tocarra was sitting in a chair next to Wahdatah's bed with her fingers interlaced with his when she felt his hand squeeze her fingers. Her heart nearly exploded with excitement.

"Oh my God! Thank you Jesus! Thank you Heavenly Father!" She screamed her praises at the top of her lungs.

ICE MIKE

"Doctor! Doctor! Hurry! Come here! He just squeezed my hand!" Tocarra screamed to the hospital staff with her backside firmly planted in the chair, not wanting to let go of his hand.

She waited for the nursing staff to show up. To her it seemed like they were taking forever.

Then Wah squeezed her hand again harder.

DEEPLY ROOTED

CHAPTER THIRTY-FOUR
Karma

Miko

Miko was feeling herself in a real way. Boss status was at the cusp of her fingertips. She could feel it! Through the dark Southeast streets, she wheeled her whip and bopped her head in rhythm to the thug music beating loudly through the speakers. Miko parked at the curb, jumped out the whip, and quickly trotted up the walkway leading to her recently fixed front door. With a twist of her key, she pushed the door open slowly before kicking off her shoes and shutting the door behind her. A pressed button on the remote filled up the house with more thug music. Piece by piece, articles of her clothing littered the floor, forming a trail of silk and lace fabric that stopped at the bathroom door.

Miko played with the water spigots until the temperature was just right. Hot steam filled the bathroom, and Miko went about readying herself for her bath. She stilled her pose when she thought she heard a noise other than the music playing outside the bathroom door. Turning the spigots off, she listened closely and crept toward the open door and glanced around. Nothing. Miko shrugged, and then turned the spigots back on. She closed the bathroom door and got comfortable. She wished a nigga would . . .

DEEPLY ROOTED

* * * * *

Tocarra

Tocarra followed Miko's car from a safe distance, careful not to let the shady bitch detect her presence. She eased up off the gas whenever necessary, and sped the BMW up when she had to. Her eyes darted over to the passenger seat, and she eyed the chrome pistol with purposeful intent. *I'll be damned if that bitch is gonna get away with this shit!* she thought, just as she turned down Miko's block. Tocarra put the whip on pause and waited for Miko to disappear inside the house. She watched through angry eyes before resting the 750 Li against the curb a few houses down from where Miko once lived with Shug.

She snatched up the pistol and made her way to the side of the house, her purse slung over her left shoulder. Tocarra tested the doorknob and smiled wickedly when it twisted. She put the tip of the pistol in the crack of the door and eased it open slowly. She managed to squeeze her voluptuous frame through the narrow opening and let out the breath she had been holding between her slightly parted lips.

Her ears adjusted to the music playing loudly throughout the house. She eyeballed the stilettos on the floor and then shut the door behind her. Scrutinizing the silk and lace clothing carefully, her eyes followed the last pieces of lingerie to the bathroom. At that point she realized the bath water was on full blast. With pistol in hand, she crept toward the bathroom and placed her hand on the knob and turned it agonizingly slow. Pinning her purse against her ribcage with her elbow, she turned the doorknob until her wrist was upside down. Steam fought desperately to escape the closed confines of the washing quarters.

Tocarra threw the door open, and her arm swung up in a murderous arc.

Bang!

The bullet hit her in the top right side of her back before travelling to her arm and making her crumble to the floor, writhing in pain. "Aaagggghhh!" she screamed in agony as her body convulsed.

"You stupid bitch! I saw your dumb ass comin' from a mile away. You square ass 'ho! Look atchu' now though, bitch!" Miko mocked the now fallen Tocarra, whose blood began to pool underneath as she tried desperately to find her bearings.

Tocarra tried to say something, but her words kept getting stuck in her throat. The shock of her gunshot wound was freezing her up.

"Awwp! Don't you say a mothafuckin' word, you silly ass bitch," Miko commanded her, waving the .380 to and fro just inches away from her face. "I'm the only one doin' any talkin' up in here," Miko gloated as she reached back and bapped Tocarra on the forehead with the butt of the gun, using all the force she could summon. Blood squirted out and Mike smiled evilly.

"How dare you step into the ring wit' a real boss bitch and expect to come out a winner! I know how those niggas think, bitch! I know how their minds work, 'ho! I don't know why they would send a square ass chick to do a goon bitch's job. Yeah, that's right. I felt it when you slapped me on the back and called yourself tagging me with that recording device. I knew what your slow poke ass was up to when you did it, bitch."

"Ungh! Ungh! Ungh!" Miko repeatedly smashed the butt of the gun into Tocarra's face with merciless brute force.

Tocarra's eyes begged for mercy when she looked up into Miko's cold, ruthless eyes. Blood from the gashes on her face trickled down and mixed with her tears.

"Where the fuck is that recorder at, bitch?" Miko struck her across the bridge of her nose and laughed when Tocarra's blood splattered onto her face. She used the back of her gun hand to wipe away the splatter, and then she licked it off the back of her fist with a wild, crazed look in her eyes.

"It ain't hard to figure your game-goofy ass out, bitch." Miko rifled through Tocarra's clothes first, and then she searched the purse that lay strewn about next to her.

"Bingo, bitch! Now it's time for us to take a ride." Miko left and returned moments later with a huge suitcase. "Get yo' ass inside, 'ho!" Her command was met with a whimper. She got on her knees next to Tocarra.

"I . . . Said . . . Get . . . Yo' . . . Ass . . . The . . . Fuck . . . In . . . Side . . . Bitch!" Miko folded the helpless Tocarra up as she spoke, half-zipping the suitcase, before standing it up straight once she smashed her into it.

The shocked and shook up Tocarra was twisted up like a pretzel inside the luggage.

Miko made a pit stop at Wahdatah's granny's house before returning home to take a much-needed shower. She had a long day ahead of her tomorrow. Plans had already been made; she had things to do and people to see.

ICE MIKE

* * * * *

Shug

"Braxton, you have a visit! Get ready. I'll be back in five minutes to get you," the deputy yelled loudly over the noise of the holding tank.

I hope that's Tocarra, Shug thought as he donned his freshest county jail outfit. The flat mattress helped maintain the comb-made creases that ran up and down the front and back of the lower half of his blue pants.

When Shug pushed past the visiting room doorway, he again scanned the crowd of mostly black and brown faces. This time he searched for Tocarra's face, hopeful that she would have some good news for him. But instead his eyes found another familiar face. His eyes frosted over with coldness. Miko stood looking stunning in a white two-piece pants suit made of Turkish wool, and an off-white silk blouse. Righteous indignation etched deep in her facial features. If looks could kill, there would have been a small massacre in the tightly spaced visiting room.

Shug stood in front of her on the other side of the three-inch thick Plexiglas with murder in his eyes, teeth grinding hard while his hateful heart beat faster with a desire to snap in half every bone in her body.

Miko smiled. She seemed to be enjoying the eye-boxing match. She genuinely got a kick out of it. The smile on her face grew wider as their eyes continued to war with one another, her body shook and shivered with pleasure. *This feel better than the sex we used to have*, she thought and wet her lips with the tip of her tongue.

The standoff was a draw, but she had every intention of winning the battle of wills and getting the last word in. It

272

was essential to her long-term plans that she got the final word in—the cherry on top when it came to fulfilling her childhood goal. A goal that was her reason to continue existing. She picked up the black phone and put it to her ear, her eyes maintaining contact with his the entire time.

Shug wanted badly to turn his back on Miko and deal with her the day he touched down, if he ever touched down. He wanted to leave her standing there stewing in her cockiness, but something deep inside was telling him not to be so hasty. Entertain the scandalous bitch and see if she would reveal any telling information. To see if she might slip up and say something that would provide him with a clue or a hint. Something that could help him get up out of this jail, so he could hunt her ass down and kill her slow and ugly at his leisure.

He picked up the phone.

"You got some nerve, bitch!" His words were so cold he could have made hot snot icicle up. He figured that by dictating the flow of the conversation it would put him at an advantage. But he was wrong. He had underestimated Miko from the jump, only he didn't know it yet.

"I know, ain't it sexy though?" She taunted him and smiled.

"I'ma kill you, Miko. On mommas, bitch. I am going to choke you to death, you scandalous ass no good 'ho!" He hissed his hatred at her.

"Punk, please. Fuck yo' mama! I murdered that bitch on my 18th birthday while you was sitting up in that youth correctional facility, so don't put shit on your mama because I already blew that bitch up!"

Words were not necessary; Shug's look said it all.

"Don't worry though. I don't plan on taking up too much of your time. I just wanted to stop by and pay you a visit. Let you know that I got this." She held up the recording device and the recorder. "So you can give up on ever thinking the police will get their hands on it."

The look on Shug's face went from one of unmasked hatred to one of obvious shock.

"Yup, that's what happens when you send a game-goofy girl to do a grown goon bitch's job."

"What the fuck did you do to Tocarra?"

"Don't trip. She's all good. Tell your vegetable ass brother that if he ever recovers from that coma, she'll be up under the lemon tree at his granny's house. Or you can go see about the bitch yourself when you get out, if you ever get out! Hahahahahaha!" Her wicked laughter would taunt Shug for the rest of his days.

"Karma's a bitch, ma'fucka. A bitch named Miko Dunbar. Please believe that!"

Miko dropped the phone and turned on the four-inch heels, leaving the scarred black phone swinging slowly side to side, hypnotizing his horror in the cruelest way imaginable.

Miko couldn't hear any of the murderous threats he yelled at the top of his lungs until his vocal cords were raw with agony. Shug was restrained by the deputies and forcefully dragged away from the visiting area.

DEEPLY ROOTED

EPILOGUE

Eighteen months later . . .

S hug did a slow duck-walk, along with the rest of the shackled line of prison-bound convicted felons. The manacles biting sharply into his skin as he looked around and savored the small window of free air between the county jail and the ominous looking prison bus waiting at the curb to take him to his new home.

The pain he felt around his wrists and ankles paled in comparison to the pain he felt from the two consecutive 25 years-to-life sentences the judge nearly broke his back with when he threw the book at him in court last week.

* * * * *

Miko leaned back in comfortable confidence as the soft Italian leather conformed to the contours of her body and hugged her voluptuous frame like a jealous lover. The two-toned black over cream-colored Rolls Royce drop head coupe on 24-inch Forgiato Plastra eight-spoke rims sailed smoothly down the Pacific Coast Highway en route to the meeting with Javier, her Columbian connect.

Her dark brown hair, tinted with light brown streaks surfed on her shoulders as the wind blew. Thoughts of the massive shipment of narcotics due to touchdown later that night danced around in her devious mind.

Miko smiled and admired the exquisite interior of the Rolls, running her fingers across the exquisite wood grain dash. "Daddy, you would be so proud of your baby girl," she said to herself. Miko reached down to the console and picked up the tall, slender glass. Touching the champagne-filled flute to her slightly parted lips, she toasted to her idol and role model, her father, the late great Kiko Dunbar.

COMING SOON . . .

DEEPLY ROOTED II

READING GROUP DISCUSSION QUESTIONS

DEEPLY ROOTED

These questions are meant to initiate discussion, provoke thought and spark debate. Your participation is appreciated and I hope my writing was pleasing to the reader in you.

1. Was Miko's conduct understandable?

2. Was Wahdatah's treatment of Carmelita warranted?

3. Did Wicked deserve to die the way he did?

4. What do you think Wahdatah and Baby Shug should have done once they were in possession of the five million dollars that their father stole?

5. How do you feel about Jracia and her situation her relationship with Wicked dealing with his death being pregnant by him being suckered into killing the wrong people and lastly her death?

6. Do you think that Tocarra brought what happened to her on herself?

7. Does Wah deserve to be in a coma?

8. Does Shug deserve to be serving a 25 years-to- life sentence in prison? Why or why not?

9. Which of the two brothers intrigued you the most? Why?

10. How did Miko's visit to her father's gravesite make you feel?

11. Do you think Miko will be a successful Queenpin?

Bio

Michael A. Davis aka Ice Mike was born and raised in San Diego, California and has been writing for 32 months. He is currently serving time in a California State Prison. To date he has penned a number of yet to be published novels including: *Dipped in Chocolate* (an erotic anthology), *Golden State Heavyweights*, *Passion Wit' A Pistol*, *Figments of my Imagination* (an urban anthology), *My Beautiful Ugly Life* (a powerful novella) and a book of poetry titled *1-4-69 Birth of a Poet*.

Ice Mike is currently hard at work penning Deeply Rooted II, the follow up to his debut novel Deeply Rooted.

If you would like to contact the author for comments, feedback or other remarks feel free to contact him at:

Michael A. Davis
#H-08904 (U-351)
PO Box 2000
Vacaville, CA 95696

COMING 2014 FROM

WAHIDA CLARK PRESENTS PUBLISHING

Butterfly by Michael A. Robinson

Enemy Bloodline by Omar Quadeer

The Ultimate Sacrifice Part 4 by Anthony
Fields

Vindicated by Tasha Macklin

Swag Part 2 by Angel Santos

The Pussy Trap 4 by Ne Ne Capri

Snake In The Grass by Bryan Pinkins

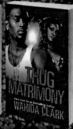

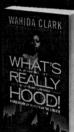

WAHIDA CLARK PRESENTS

SWAG

A NOVEL BY

ANGEL SANTOS

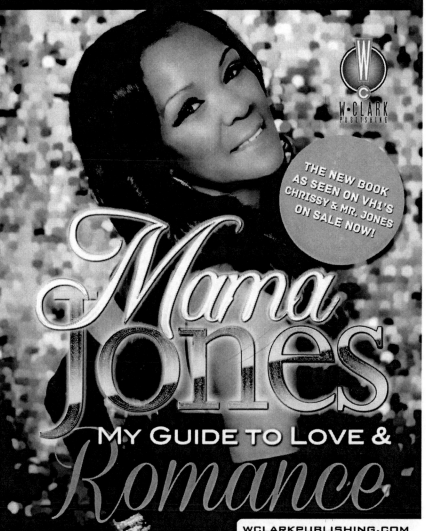

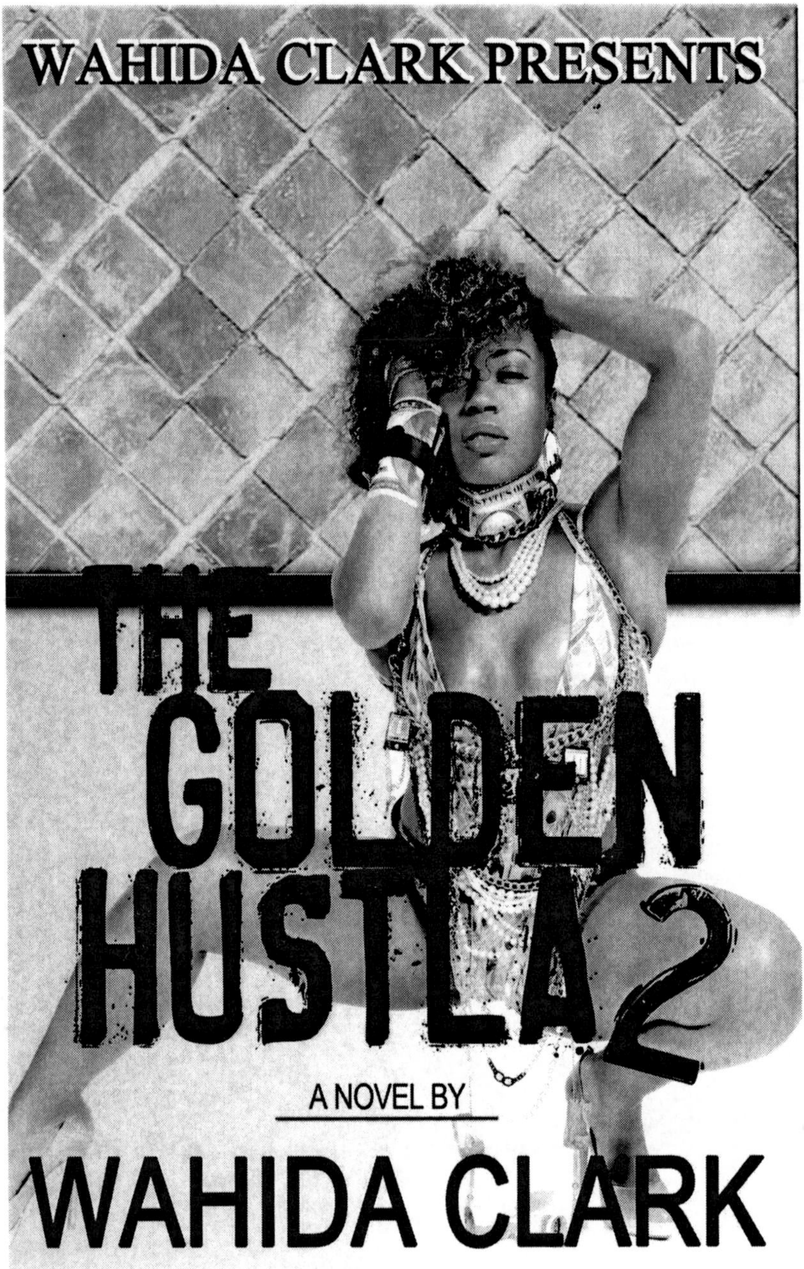
WAHIDA CLARK PRESENTS
THE
GOLDEN
HUSTLA 2
A NOVEL BY
WAHIDA CLARK

CPSIA information can be obtained at www.ICGtesting.com
Printed in the USA
LVOW06s0757260514

387280LV00019B/946/P